W9-ARD-443

FIND ME

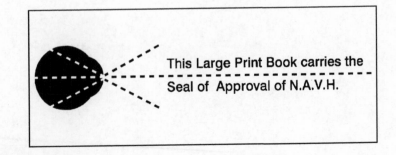

FIND ME

ANDRÉ ACIMAN

THORNDIKE PRESS
A part of Gale, a Cengage Company

Copyright 2019 by André Aciman.
Thorndike Press, a part of Gale, a Cengage Company.

ALL RIGHTS RESERVED
Thorndike Press® Large Print Basic.
The text of this Large Print edition is unabridged.
Other aspects of the book may vary from the original edition.
Set in 16 pt. Plantin.

**LIBRARY OF CONGRESS CIP DATA ON FILE.
CATALOGUING IN PUBLICATION FOR THIS BOOK
IS AVAILABLE FROM THE LIBRARY OF CONGRESS**

ISBN-13: 978-1-4328-7636-4 (hardcover alk. paper)

Published in 2020 by arrangement with Farrar, Straus and Giroux

Printed in Mexico
Print Number: 01   Print Year: 2020

Para mis tres hijos

TEMPO

Why so glum?

I watched her get on at the station in Florence. She slid open the glass door and, once inside the car, looked around, then right away dumped her backpack on the empty seat next to mine. She took off her leather jacket, put down the English-language paperback she was reading, then placed a square white box on the luggage rack and threw herself onto the seat diagonally across from mine in what seemed a restless, ill-tempered huff. She reminded me of someone who'd just had a heated argument seconds before boarding and was still stewing over the cutting words either she or someone else had spoken before hanging up. Her dog, which she was trying to keep tucked between her ankles while holding a red leash looped around her fist, seemed no less jittery than she was. "*Buona,* good girl," she finally said, hoping to calm it down, *"buona,"* she repeated, as the dog still fidgeted and tried to squirm out of the firm grip. The presence of the dog annoyed me, and instinctively I refused to uncross my legs or budge to make room for it. But she didn't seem to notice either me or my body language. Instead, she immediately rummaged through the backpack, found a slim plastic bag, and took out two tiny bone-shaped treats for the dog, then laid them in her palm and watched the dog lick them off. *"Brava."* With the dog momentarily placated, she half lifted herself to fix her shirt, shifted in her seat once or twice, then slumped into a sort of upset stupor, staring out indifferently at Florence as the train began to pull out of the Santa Maria Novella station. She was still stewing and, perhaps without noticing, shook her head, once, twice, obviously still cussing whomever she'd quarreled with before boarding. For a moment she looked so totally forlorn that, while staring at my open book, I caught myself struggling to come up with something to say, if only to help defuse what had all the bearings of a gathering storm about to erupt in our little corner at the very end of the car. Then I thought twice about it. Better to leave her alone and go on with my reading. But when I caught her looking at

me, I couldn't help myself: "Why so glum?"
I asked.

Only then did it occur to me how thoroughly inappropriate my question must have sounded to a complete stranger on a train, to say nothing of one who seemed ready to explode at the slightest provocation. All she did was stare at me with a baffled, hostile glint in her eyes that presaged the very words about to cut me down and put me in my place. *Mind your own business, old man.* Or: *What's it to you, anyway?* Or she'd make a face and utter a withering rebuke: *Jerk!*

"No, not glum, just thinking," she said.

I was so taken aback by the gentle, almost rueful tone of her reply that I was left more speechless than if she had told me to fuck off.

"Maybe thinking makes me look glum."

"So yours are happy thoughts?"

"No, not happy either," she replied.

I smiled but said nothing, already regretting my shallow, patronizing banter.

"But maybe glum after all," she added, conceding the point with a subdued laugh.

I apologized for sounding tactless.

"No need," she said, already scanning the beginnings of the countryside outside the window. Was she American, I asked. She was. "Me too," I said. "I could tell from your accent," she added with a smile. I explained that I'd been living in Italy for almost thirty years, but couldn't for the life of me undo the accent. When I asked, she replied she had settled in Italy with her parents when she was twelve.

We were both headed for Rome. "For work?" I asked.

"No, not work. It's my father. He's not well." Then, raising her eyes at me: "Might explain the glumness, I suppose."

"Is it serious?"

"I think so."

"I'm sorry," I said.

She shrugged her shoulders. "Life!"

Then, changing her tone: "And you? Business or pleasure?"

I smiled at the mock-formulaic question and explained that I had been invited to give a reading to university students. But I was also meeting my son, who lived in Rome and was picking me up at the station.

"Surely a sweet boy."

I could tell she was being facetious. But I liked her breezy, informal manner that skidded from sullen to sprightly and assumed mine did as well. Her tone jibed with her casual clothes: scuffed hiking boots, a pair of jeans, no makeup, and a half-unbuttoned, faded, reddish lumberjack shirt worn over a black T-shirt. And yet, despite the rumpled look, she had green eyes and dark eyebrows. She knows, I thought, she knows. Probably knows why I made that silly comment about her glumness. I was sure strangers were always finding one pretext or another to start a conversation with her. Which explains that irritated *don't you even try* look she projects wherever she goes.

After her ironic comment about my son, I was not surprised to find our conversation lagging. Time to pick up our respective books. But then she turned to me and asked point-blank: "Are you excited about seeing your son?" Again, I thought she was ribbing me somehow, but her tone was not flippant. There was something at once alluring and disarming in the way she got personal and cut straight through the hurdles between strangers on a train. I liked it. Perhaps she wanted to know what a man almost twice her age felt before meeting his son. Or perhaps she simply didn't feel like reading. She was waiting for me to answer. "So, are you happy — maybe? Nervous — maybe?"

"Not really nervous, or just a bit, perhaps," I said. "A parent is always scared of being an imposition, to say nothing of a bore."

"You think you're a bore?"

I loved that what I'd just said had caught her by surprise.

"Maybe I am. But then, let's face it, who isn't."

"I don't think my father is a bore."

Had I perhaps offended her? "Then I take it back," I said.

She looked at me and smiled. "Not so fast."

She prods, then drills right through you. In this, she reminded me of my son — she was slightly older, but had the same ability to call out all my gaffes and cagey little ploys, leaving me scuttled after we'd argued and made up.

What kind of person are you when someone gets to know you? I wanted to ask. *Are you funny, jovial, playful, or is there a glum, ill-tempered serum coursing in your veins that clouds your features and blots out all the laughter promised by that smile and those green eyes?* I wanted to know — because I couldn't tell.

I was about to compliment her on her ability to read people so well when her phone rang. *Boyfriend, of course! What else.* I'd grown so used to constant cell phone interruptions, that it was no longer possible for me to meet students over coffee or talk to my colleagues or to my son even without

14

a mobile phone call barging in. Saved by the phone, silenced by the phone, shunted by the phone.

"Hi, Pa," she said as soon as it rang. I believed she was picking up the phone right away to prevent the loud chime from disturbing other passengers. But what surprised me was how she yelled into her phone. "It's the damned train. It stopped, I've no idea for how long, but should be no more than two hours. See you soon." The father was asking her something. "Of course I did, you old goon, how could I forget." He asked something else. "That too." Silence. "Me too. Lots and lots."

She clicked off the phone and tossed it into her backpack, as if to say: *We're not going to be interrupted again.* She gave me an uneasy smile. "Parents," she finally said, meaning *The same everywhere, aren't they?*

But then she explained. "I see him every weekend — I'm his weekend wallah — my siblings and his caregiver take care of him weekdays." Before giving me a chance to say another word, she asked, "So, did you prettify yourself for tonight's event?"

What a way to describe what I wore! "Do I look *prettified*?" I replied, bandying the word back at her in jest so she'd not think I was fishing for compliments.

15

"Well, the pocket square, the well-pressed shirt, no tie, but then the cuff links? I'd say you gave it some thought. Old-school a bit, but dapper."

We both smiled.

"Actually, I have this," I said, half removing a colorful necktie from my jacket pocket and slipping it back in. I wanted her to see that I had enough of a sense of humor to poke fun at myself.

"Just as I thought," she said. "Prettified! Not like a retired professor in Sunday clothes, but almost. So, what do the two of you do in Rome?"

Was she ever going to let up? Had I started something with my initial question that made her think we could be so informal? "We meet every five or six weeks. He's been living in Rome but will soon be moving to Paris. I miss him already. I like spending the day with him; we do nothing, really, mostly walk, though it usually turns out to be the same walk: his Rome, by the conservatory, my Rome, where I used to live as a young teacher. Eventually we'll always have lunch at Armando's. He puts up with me or maybe he enjoys my company, I still can't tell, maybe both, but we've ritualized these visits: Via Vittoria, Via Belsiana, Via del Babuino. Sometimes we wander off all the way to the Protestant Cemetery. They're like the markers of our lives. We've nicknamed them our vigils after the way pious people stop at various *madonnelle* — street shrines — to pay homage to the Madonna of the street. Neither of us forgets: lunch, walk, vigils. I'm lucky. Walking around Rome with him is itself a vigil. Everywhere you turn you stumble on memories — your own, someone else's, the city's. I like Rome at twilight, he likes it afternoons, and there've been times when we'll have an afternoon tea anywhere just to drag things out a bit till evening sets in and we have drinks."

"And that's it?"

"That's it. We'll walk Via Margutta for me, then Via Belsiana for him — old loves in both our cases."

"Vigils of past vigils?" joked the young woman on the train. "Is he married?"

"No."

"Does he have someone?"

"I don't know. I suspect there must be someone. But I do worry about him. There was someone quite a while back and I did ask if there was anyone now, but all he did was shake his head and say, 'Don't ask, Papa, don't ask.' It meant no one or everyone, and I couldn't tell which was worse. He used to be so open with me."

"I think he was being honest with you."

"Yes, in a way."

"I like him," said the young woman sitting diagonally across from me. "Maybe because I'm very much the same. Sometimes I'm blamed for being too open, too forward, and then for being too guarded and withdrawn."

"I don't think he's withdrawn with others. But I don't think he's very happy."

"I know how he feels."

"Isn't there someone in your life?"

"If you only knew."

"What?" I asked. The word sprang out of me like a surprised and doleful sigh. What could she mean — that there was no one in her life, or that there were too many, or that the man in her life had walked out on her and left her devastated with nothing but an urge to take out her anger on herself or on a succession of beaux? Or did people simply come and go, come and go, as I feared so many did with my own son — or was she the sort who slips in and out of people's lives without leaving a trace or a keepsake?

"I don't know if I'm the type who even likes people, much less falls in love with them."

I could just see it in the two of them: the same embittered, impassive, injured hearts.

"Is it that you don't like people, or that

18

you just grow tired of them and can't for the life of you remember why you ever found them interesting?"

She was suddenly quiet, looked totally startled, and didn't utter a word. Her eyes stared straight at me. Had I offended her again? "How could you have known that?" she finally asked. This was the first time I'd seen her turn serious and look cross. I could see her whetting some well-honed words with which to cut down my presumptuous meddling into her private life. I shouldn't have said anything. "We've met no more than fifteen minutes ago, and yet you know me! How could you have known this about me?" Then, catching herself: "How much do you charge an hour?"

"On the house. But if I know anything it's because I think we're all like that. Plus, you're young and you're beautiful, and I'm sure men gravitate to you all the time, so it's not that you have a hard time meeting someone."

Had I once again spoken out of turn and crossed a line?

To walk back the compliment, I added, "It's just that the magic of someone new never lasts long enough. We only want those we can't have. It's those we lost or who never knew we existed who leave their mark.

The others barely echo."

"Is this the case with Miss Margutta?" she asked.

This woman doesn't miss a beat, I thought. I liked the name Miss Margutta. It cast whatever existed years ago between us in a mild and docile, almost laughable light.

"I'll never really know. We were together for so short a while and it happened so fast."

"How long ago?"

I thought for a moment.

"I'm ashamed to say."

"Oh, just say it!"

"At least two decades. Well, almost three."

"And?"

"We met at a party when I was a teacher in Rome at the time. She was with someone, I was with someone, we happened to speak, and neither wished to stop. Eventually she and her boyfriend left the party, and soon after, we left as well. We didn't even exchange numbers. But I couldn't put her out of my mind. So I called the friend who'd invited me to the party and asked if he had her phone number. And here is the joke. A day earlier, she'd called him to ask for *my* phone number. 'I heard you were looking for me,' I said when I finally called her. I should have introduced myself, but I wasn't really thinking, I was nervous.

"She recognized my voice right away, or perhaps our friend had already warned her. 'I was going to call you,' she said. 'But you didn't,' I replied. 'No, I didn't.' Which is when she said something that showed she had more courage than I and it sent my pulse racing, because I didn't expect it and will never forget it. 'So, how do we do this?' she asked. *How do we do this?* With that one sentence I knew my life was being pushed out of its familiar orbit. No one I knew had ever directed such frank, almost feral words at me."

"I like her."

"What was there not to like. Blunt and forward, and so to-the-point that I had to make a decision right then and there. 'Let's have lunch,' I said. 'Because dinner is difficult, right?' she asked. I loved the bold, implicit irony in what she'd said. 'Let's have lunch — as in today,' I said. 'As in today it is.' We laughed at the speed with which things were happening. Lunch, that day, was scarcely an hour away."

"Did it bother you that she meant to cheat on her boyfriend?"

"No. Nor did it bother me that I was doing the same thing. The lunch lasted a long time. I walked her to her home on Via Margutta, then she walked me back to where we'd had lunch, and then I walked her back to her home again.

" 'Tomorrow?' I asked, still uncertain whether I wasn't pushing things. 'Absolutely, tomorrow.' It was the week before Christmas. By Tuesday afternoon we did something totally crazy: we bought two plane tickets and flew to London."

"So romantic!"

"Everything went so fast and felt so natural, that neither saw the need to discuss the matter with our partners or give them a second thought. We simply let go all our inhibitions. In those days we still had inhibitions."

"You mean unlike today?"

"I wouldn't know."

"No, I suppose you wouldn't."

Her oblique taunt let me know I was meant to be slightly riled.

I chuckled.

She did as well, her way of signaling that she knew I was being disingenuous.

"In any event, it ended right away. She went back to her boyfriend, and I to my girlfriend. We did not remain friends. But I attended their wedding, and eventually I invited them to ours. They stayed married. We didn't. *Voilà*."

"Why did you let her go back to her

boyfriend?"

"Why? Perhaps because I was never totally persuaded by my feelings. I just didn't fight to keep her, which she already knew I wouldn't. Perhaps I wanted to be in love and feared I wasn't and preferred our little limbo in London to facing up to what I didn't feel for her. Perhaps I preferred to doubt rather than know. So how much do *you* charge per hour?"

"Touché!"

When was the last time I'd spoken to someone like this?

"So tell me about the person in *your* life," I said. "I'm sure you're seeing someone special right now?"

"Seeing someone, yes."

"For how long?" Then I stopped short. "If I may ask."

"You may ask. Barely four months." Then, shrugging her shoulders: "Doesn't merit writing home about."

"Do you like him?"

"I like him fine. We get along. And we like many of the same things. But we're just two roommates pretending to have a life together. We don't."

"What a way to put it. *Two roommates pretending to have a life together.* Sad."

"It is sad. But what's also sad is that, in

23

these past few moments, I may have shared more with you than in a whole week with him."

"Maybe you're not the kind who opens up to people."

"But I'm speaking with you."

"I'm a stranger, and with strangers opening up is easy."

"The only ones I can speak frankly with are my father and Pavlova, my dog, and neither is going to be around much longer. Besides, my father hates my current boyfriend."

"Not so unusual for a father."

"Actually, he worshipped my previous boyfriend."

"Did you?"

She smiled, already anticipating that she'd toss off her answer with a dash of humor: "No, I didn't." She thought for a moment. "My previous boyfriend wanted to marry me. I told him no. I was so relieved that he didn't make a fuss when we broke up. Then not six months later, I heard he was getting married. I was livid. If I was ever hurt and cried for love it was on the day I heard he was marrying a woman we had spent hours and months making fun of when we were together."

Silence.

"Jealous without being the slightest bit in love — you are difficult," I finally said.

She gave me a look that was at once veiled reproof for daring to speak this way about her and bewildered curiosity that wished to know more. "I've known you for less than an hour on a train. And yet you totally understand me. I like it. But I might as well tell you of this other, terrible defect."

"What now?"

We both laughed.

"I never stay close with anyone I've had a relationship with. Most people don't like to burn bridges. I seem to blow them up — probably because there wasn't much of a bridge to start with. Sometimes I leave everything behind in their apartment and simply disappear. I hate the drawn-out process of packing up and moving out and those unavoidable postmortems that turn into teary-eyed pleas to stay together; above all I hate the lingering pretense of an attachment after we don't even want to be touched by someone we no longer recall wanting to sleep with. You're right: I don't know why I start with anyone. The sheer annoyance of a new relationship. Plus the small home habits I need to put up with. The smell of his birdcage. The way he likes his CDs stacked. The sound of an ancient radiator in the middle of the night that wakes me but never him. He wants to shut the windows. I like them open. I'll drop my clothes wherever; he wants our towels folded and put away. He likes the tube of toothpaste squeezed neatly from the bottom up; I squeeze it whatever way I can and always lose the cap, which he always finds somewhere on the floor behind the toilet bowl. The remote control has its place, the milk needs to stand close but not too close to the freezer, underwear and socks belong in *this* drawer but not *that* drawer.

"And yet, I'm not difficult. I'm actually a good person, just a bit opinionated. But it's only a front. I put up with everyone and everything. At least for a while. Then one day it just hits me: I don't want to be with this guy, don't want him near me, need to get away. I fight this feeling. But as soon as a man senses this, he'll hound me with despairing puppy eyes. Once I spot that look, pfffff, I'm gone and immediately find someone else.

"Men!" she finally said, as though that one word summed up all the shortcomings most women are willing to overlook and learn to put up with and ultimately forgive in the men they hope to love for the rest of their lives even when they know they won't. "I hate to see anyone hurt."

A shadow hovered over her features. I wished I could touch her face, gently. She caught the glance, I lowered my eyes.

Once again, I noticed her boots. Wild, untamed boots, as though they'd been dragged on craggy treks and acquired an aged, weatherworn look, which meant she trusted them. She liked her things worn and broken in. She liked comfort. Her thick navy woolen socks were men's socks, probably lifted from the drawer of the man she claimed she had no love for. But the mid-season leather biker's jacket looked very expensive. Prada, most likely. Had she dashed out of her boyfriend's home, and in her hurry, thrown on the first items at hand with a hasty *I'm heading out to my dad's, call you this evening*? She was wearing a man's watch. His too? Or did she just prefer men's watches? Everything about her suggested something gritty, rugged, unfinished. And then I caught a sliver of skin between her socks and the cuff of her jeans — she had the smoothest ankles.

"Tell me about your father," I said.

"My father? He's not doing well, and we're losing him." Then she interrupted herself: "Do you still charge by the hour?"

"As I said, confiding comes easier between strangers who'll never meet again."

"You think so?"

"What, confiding on a train?"

"No, that we'll never meet again?"

"What are the chances?"

"True, very true."

We exchanged smiles.

"So go on about your father."

"I've been thinking about this. My love for him has changed. It's no longer a spontaneous love, but a brooding, cautious, caregiver's love. Not the real deal. Still, we are very open with each other, and there is nothing I'm ashamed to tell him. My mother left almost two decades ago, and since then it's been just him and me. He had a girlfriend for a while, but now he lives alone. Someone comes to take care of him, cooks, does his laundry, cleans and tidies up. Today is his seventy-sixth birthday. Hence the cake," she said, pointing to the square white box resting on the top bin. She seemed embarrassed by it, which may be why she threw in a tiny giggle when she pointed to it. "He said he invited two friends for lunch, but he still hasn't heard from them, and my guess is they won't show up, no one does these days. Neither will my siblings. He likes profiteroles from an old shop not far from where I live in Florence. It reminds him of better days when he used to teach there once. He shouldn't have anything sweet of course, but . . ."

She didn't need to finish the sentence.

The silence between us lasted awhile. Once again I made a motion to pick up my book, convinced we were done talking this time. A bit later, with my book still open, I started looking out at the rolling Tuscan landscape and my mind began to drift. An odd and shapeless thought about how she'd changed seats and was now sitting next to me began to settle on my mind. I knew I was dozing off.

"You're not reading," she said. Then, seeing she might have disturbed me, she immediately added, "I can't either."

"Tired of reading," I said, "can't focus."

"Is it interesting?" she finally asked, looking at the cover of my book.

"It's not bad. Rereading Dostoyevsky after many years can be a bit disappointing."

"Why?"

"Have you read Dostoyevsky?"

"Yes. I adored him when I was fifteen."

"So did I. His vision of life is one that an adolescent can immediately grasp: tormented, filled with contradictions, and lots of bile, venom, shame, love, pity, sorrow, and spite, and the most disarming acts of kindness and self-sacrifice — all of it so unevenly thrust together. To the adolescent I was, Dostoyevsky was my introduction to complex psychology. I thought I was a thoroughly confused person — but all his characters were no less confused. I felt at home. My sense is that one learns more about the blotchy makeup of human psychology from Dostoyevsky than from Freud, or any psychiatrist for that matter."

She was silent.

"I see a shrink," she finally said, with an almost audible rise of protest in her voice.

Had I yet again snubbed her without meaning to?

"I see one too," I rejoindered, perhaps to take back what might have seemed an unintended slight.

We stared at each other. I liked her warm and trusting smile; it suggested something frail and genuine, perhaps even vulnerable. No wonder the men in her life closed in on her. They knew what they were losing the moment she turned her eyes away. Out went the smile, or the languor when she asked heart-to-heart questions while staring with those piercing green eyes that never let up, out the disquieting need for intimacy that her glance tore out of every man when your eyes happened to lock on her in a public space and you knew *there went your life.* She was doing it right now. She made intimacy want to happen, made it easy, as if you'd always had it in you to give, and were craving to share it but realized you'd never find it in yourself unless it was with her. I wanted to hold her, touch her hand, let a finger drift along her forehead.

"So why the shrink?" she asked, as though she had pondered the idea and found it totally bewildering. "If I may ask," she added, smiling as she parodied my own words. Obviously she wasn't used to a softer, more congenial approach when speaking to a stranger. I asked why she was surprised I was seeing a shrink.

"Because you look so settled, so — prettified."

"Hard to say. Maybe because the empty spaces of adolescence when I discovered Dostoyevsky never got filled. I once believed they'd be filled at some point; now I am not sure such spaces are ever filled. Still, I want to understand. Some of us never jumped to the next level. We lost track of where we were headed and as a result stayed where we started."

"So this is why you're rereading Dostoyevsky?"

I smiled at the aptness of the question. "Perhaps because I am always trying to retrace my steps back to a spot where I should have jumped on the ferryboat headed to the other bank called life but ended up dawdling on the wrong wharf or, with my luck, took the wrong ferryboat altogether. It's all an older man's game, you know."

"You don't sound like the sort of person who takes the wrong ferry. Did you?"

Was she teasing me?

"I was thinking of this when I boarded the train in Genoa this morning, because it occurred to me that perhaps there were one or two ferryboats I should have sailed on instead and never did."

"Why didn't you?"

I shook my head then shrugged my shoulders to suggest I didn't know why or didn't want to say.

"Aren't those the absolute worst scenarios: the things that might have happened but never did and might still happen though we've given up hoping they could."

I must have looked at her with totally baffled eyes. "Where did you ever learn to think this way?"

"I read a lot." Then, with a self-conscious glance: "I like talking to you." She paused a moment. "So, was your marriage the wrong ferryboat?"

This woman was brilliant. And she was beautiful. And she thought along the same twisted, meandering paths I took sometimes.

"At first, no," I replied, "or at least I didn't want to see it that way. But after our son left for the States there was so little between us that it felt as though his entire childhood was nothing more than a dress rehearsal for our unavoidable separation. We barely talked and when we did, it seemed we seldom spoke the same language. We were exceptionally cordial and kind, but even when we were in the same room we felt so alone together. We'd sit at the same dining table, but weren't eating together, slept in the same bed but not together, watched the same programs, traveled to the same cities, shared the same yoga instructor, laughed at the same jokes but never together, and sat side by side at crowded movie theaters, but never rubbed elbows. There came a time when I'd spot two lovers kissing on the street or even hugging and didn't know why they were kissing. We were alone together — until one day one of us broke the pickle dish."

"Pickle dish?"

"Sorry, Edith Wharton. She left me for

someone who was my best friend, and who is still my friend. The irony is that I wasn't in the least bit sorry she'd found someone."

"Maybe because it freed you to find someone else."

"I never did. We stayed good friends, and I know she worries about me."

"Should she?"

"No. So, why the shrink?" I asked, eager to change the subject.

"Me? Loneliness. I can't stand being by myself yet I can't wait to be alone. Look at me. I am alone here on a train, happy to be with my book, away from a man I won't ever love, but I would much rather talk to a stranger. No offense, I hope."

I smiled back: *None taken.*

"I tend to talk to everyone these days, I start conversations with the mailman just to gab a bit, but never tell my boyfriend how I feel, what I read, what I want, what I hate. In any event, he wouldn't listen, much less understand. He has no sense of humor. I need to explain every punch line to him."

We continued chatting until the conductor came to collect our tickets. He looked at the dog, complained that dogs weren't allowed on the train except in cages.

"So what am I supposed to do?" she snapped back. "Throw her overboard?

34

Pretend I'm blind? Or get off now and miss my father's seventy-sixth birthday party which won't really be a party because it's his very last since he's actually dying? Just tell me."

The conductor wished her a good day.

"Anche a Lei," she muttered. And to you too. Then, turning to her dog: "And stop drawing attention to yourself!"

Then my phone rang. I was tempted to stand up and take the call in the empty spot between the cars, but decided to stay put. The dog, stirred by the chime, was now staring at me with gaping, quizzical eyes as if to say, *You too with the phone, now?*

My son, I mouthed to my companion, who smiled at me and then, without asking, took advantage of the sudden interruption to gesture she was going to the bathroom. She handed me the leash and whispered, "She won't be any trouble."

I looked at her when she stood up and, for the first time, realized that her rough-hewn look wasn't as dressed down as I'd initially thought, and that she was, once she stood up, more attractive yet. Had I noticed this earlier and tried to brush the thought away? Or had I really been blind? It would have pleased me no end had my son seen me stepping off the train in her company. I knew we'd be talking about her on our way to Armando's. I could even foresee how he'd start the conversation: *So tell me about that model type you were chitchatting with at Termini . . .*

But then just as I was fantasizing his reaction, the phone call changed everything. He was calling to say he was not going to be able to meet me at all that day. I gasped a plaintive *Why?* He was replacing a pianist who'd fallen ill and had a recital in Naples that same day. When would he be back? Tomorrow, he said. I loved hearing his voice. What was he playing? Mozart, all Mozart. Meanwhile my companion returned from the bathroom and silently resumed her seat across from me, leaning forward, which signaled she meant to continue speaking after I'd hung up. I stared at her more intensely than I'd done during our entire trip, partly because I was busy with someone else on the phone, which gave my glance a vaguely inattentive, guileless, roaming air, but also because it allowed me to keep staring at those eyes that were so used to being stared at and that liked being stared at, and might never have guessed that if I found the courage to return her gaze as fiercely as hers was at that moment it was also because, in staring, I'd begun to nurse the impression that in her eyes mine were just as beautiful.

Definitely an older man's fantasy.

There was a halt in my conversation with my son. "But I was so counting on taking a long walk with you. This is why I took the earlier train. I came for you, not for the paltry reading." I was disappointed but I also knew that I had my companion as an audience, and perhaps I was hamming it up a bit for her as well. Then, realizing I had gone too far with my complaint, I caught myself: "But I understand. I do." The girl seated diagonally in front of me cast an anxious look in my direction. Then she shrugged her shoulders, not to display her indifference to what was happening between me and my son, but to tell me, or so I thought, to leave the poor boy alone — *Don't make him feel guilty.* To the shrug she added a gesture with her left hand to suggest I should *just let it go, get over it.* "So tomorrow?" I asked. Would he come and pick me up at the hotel? Midafternoon, he replied — fourish? "Fourish," I said. "Vigils," he said. "Vigils," I replied.

"You've heard him," I finally said, turning to her.

"I heard *you.*"

She was taunting me again. And she was

smiling. A side of me thought she'd leaned even more toward me and had thought of standing up to move to the seat next to me and put both hands in mine. Had this crossed her mind and was I seizing on her wish to do so, or was I simply making it up because the wish was in me?

"I was looking forward to our lunch. I wanted to laugh with him and hear about his life, his recitals, his career. I was even hoping to spot him before he spotted me and that he'd find a moment to meet you."

"It's not the end of the world. You'll see him tomorrow *fourish*?" Yet again, I caught the jeer in her voice. And I loved it.

"The irony, however —" I started to add, but then changed my mind.

"The irony, however?" she inquired. *She doesn't let go, does she*, I thought.

I was silent for a moment.

"The irony is that I'm not sorry he's not coming today. I have quite a bit to do before the reading and maybe I could use a rest at the hotel instead of walking about the city as we normally do when I'm just visiting him."

"Why should that surprise you? You lead separate lives, regardless of how they intersect or how many vigils the two of you share."

38

I liked what she had just said. It didn't reveal anything I didn't already know, but it showed a degree of thoughtfulness and care that surprised me and didn't seem to fit the person who'd sat down in a huff on boarding the train.

"How do *you* know so much?" I asked, feeling emboldened and staring at her.

She smiled.

"To quote someone I met on a train once: 'We're all this way.' "

She liked this as much as I did.

As we neared the Rome station, our train began to stall. Minutes later, it stirred again. "I'm taking a taxi when we get to the station," she said.

"It's what I'm doing."

It turned out her father's home was five minutes away from my hotel. He lived along the Lungotevere and I was staying on Via Garibaldi, just a few steps from where I used to live years ago.

"Split a cab, then," she said.

We heard the announcement of Roma Termini, and as the train crawled toward the station, we watched row upon row of shabby buildings and travertine warehouses come into view, each displaying old billboards and faded, dirty colors. Not the Rome I loved. The sight unsettled me and made me feel ambivalent about the visit and the reading and the prospect of being back in a place that already stored too many memories, some good, most less so. Suddenly, I resolved that I'd give my reading that evening, have my de rigueur cocktail with old colleagues, then find a way to duck the usual dinner invitation, and come up with something to do by myself, maybe catch a film, and then stay indoors the next day till my son dropped by at four. "At least I hope they booked the room with the large balcony and the view of all the domes," I said. I wanted to show, despite my son's phone call, that I knew how to look at the brighter side of things. "I'll check in, wash my hands, find a good place to have lunch, then rest."

"Why? Don't you like cake?" she asked.

"I like cake fine. Can you suggest a good spot for lunch?"

"Yes."

"Where?"

"My father's. Come for lunch. Our home couldn't be closer to your hotel."

I smiled, truly moved by the spontaneous offer. She was feeling sorry for me.

"That's very sweet of you. But I really shouldn't. Your father is having a cherished moment with the person he loves the most and you want me to crash his party? Plus, he doesn't know me from Adam."

"But I know you," she said, as though this would change my mind.

"You don't even know my name."

"Didn't you say Adam?"

We both laughed. "Samuel."

"Please come. It will be very simple and low-key, I promise."

Still, I couldn't accept.

"Just say yes."

"I can't."

The train had finally arrived. She picked up her jacket and her book, shouldered her backpack, wrapped the dog leash around her hand, and took down the white box from the upper bin. "This is the cake," she finally said. "Oh, just say yes."

I shook my head to convey a deferential but determined no.

"Here's what I propose. I'll pick out a fish and leafy greens on Campo de' Fiori — I always buy fish, cook fish, eat fish — and before you know it, I'll throw together an amazing lunch in no more than twenty minutes. He'll be happy to see someone new at the door."

"What makes you think he and I will have anything to say to each other? It could be terribly awkward. Besides, what do you suppose he's going to think?"

It took her a moment to catch on.

"He won't think that at all," she finally said.

Clearly, it hadn't even crossed her mind.

"Besides," she added, "I'm old enough, and he's old enough to think whatever."

A moment of silence elapsed as we stepped off the train and landed on the crowded platform. I couldn't help but give a hasty and discreet look around. Perhaps my son had changed his mind and meant to surprise me after all. But no one was waiting for me on the platform.

"Listen" — it suddenly occurred to me — "and I don't even know your name —"

"Miranda."

The name struck me. "Listen, Miranda, it's really lovely of you to invite me, but —"

"We're strangers on a train, Sami, and I know talk is cheap," she said, already fabricating a nickname for me, "but I've opened up to you and you've opened up to me. I don't think either of us knows many people with whom we've been so casually honest. Let's not make this the stereotypical moment that happens on a train and then stays on the train like an umbrella or a forgotten pair of gloves left behind somewhere. I know I'll regret it. Plus, it would make me,

Miranda, very happy."

I loved how she'd said this.

There was a moment of silence. I wasn't hesitating, but I could right away tell she had interpreted my silence as acquiescence. Before picking up her phone to call her father, she asked if I didn't have to make a phone call as well, perhaps? Her *perhaps* moved me, but I wasn't sure why or what precisely it suggested, nor did I want to speculate and be proven wrong. *This girl thinks of everything,* I thought. I shook my head. I didn't have anyone to call.

"Pa. I'm bringing a guest," she shouted into her phone. He mustn't have heard. "A guest," she repeated. Then, trying to keep the dog from jumping on me: "What do you mean *what kind of guest*? A guest. He's a professor. Like you." She turned to me to make sure she had inferred correctly. I nodded. Then the answer to the obvious question: "No, you're totally wrong. I'm bringing fish. Twenty minutes absolute max, I promise.

"This should give him time to put on clean clothes," she joked.

Would she ever suspect that if I had already resolved to cancel dinner with colleagues tonight it was because, without quite admitting it to myself, I was already coddling the distant hope of having dinner with her instead? How would that ever come about?

When we finally arrived on the corner of Ponte Sisto, I asked the driver to stop. "Why don't I drop my bag in my room and join you at your dad's — say in ten minutes."

But she grabbed my left arm as the car was about to stop. "Absolutely not. If you're anything like me you'll check into your hotel, drop your bag in your room, wash your hands, which you said you're so eager to do, and then after letting a good fifteen minutes pass, you'll call to say you've changed your mind and decided you can't come. Or you might not call at all. Maybe, if you're anything like me, you'll even find the right words to wish my father a happy birthday and mean it as well. Aren't you like me?"

This too moved me.

"Maybe."

"Then if you're really anything like me you probably like being found out, admit it."

"If you're anything like me you're already wondering *Why did I even invite this fellow?*"

"Then I'm not like you."

We both laughed.

When was the last time?

44

"What?" she asked.

"Nothing."

"Right!"

Had she read this too?

When we got out, we rushed to Campo de' Fiori, where we found her fish vendor's stand. Before ordering, she asked me to hold the leash. I was reluctant to approach the stand with the dog, but they knew her there, and she said it wasn't a problem. "What kind of fish do you like?" "The easiest to cook," I replied. "How about some scallops as well, they seem to have plenty today — Are they from today's catch?" she asked. "This dawn," replied the vendor. "Are you sure?" "Of course I am sure." They'd been doing this for years. As she leaned over to inspect the scallops, I caught sight of her back. I had an impulse to put an arm around her waist, her shoulders, and kiss her on her neck and face. I looked away and instead eyed the liquor store across from the stand. "Would your father like a dry white from Friuli?"

"He shouldn't drink wine, but I'd love a dry white from anywhere."

"I'll get a Sancerre as well."

"You're not planning on killing my father, are you?"

When the fish and the scallops were

wrapped, she remembered the vegetables. On our way to a nearby store, I couldn't resist: "Why me?"

"Why me what?"

"Why are you inviting *me*?"

"Because you like trains, because you were stood up today, because you ask too many questions, because I want to know you better. Is that so difficult?" she said. I didn't press her to explain. Perhaps I didn't want to hear that she liked me no more, no less than she liked scallops or leafy greens.

She found spinach, I spotted small persimmons, touched, then sniffed them, and saw that they were ripe. It was, I said, the first time this year that I'd be eating persimmons.

"Then you have to make a wish."

"What do you mean?"

She affected exasperation. "Every time you eat a fruit for the first time that year you need to make a wish. I'm surprised you didn't know that."

I thought for a few seconds. "I can't think of a wish."

"Some life," she said, meaning either that my life was so enviably put together that there was nothing left to wish for — or that it was so hopelessly bereft of joy that wishing something was a luxury no longer worth

46

considering.

"You have to wish. Think harder."

"Can I yield my wish to you?"

"I've already had my wish."

"When?"

"In the taxi."

"What was it?"

"How quickly we forget: that you'd come for lunch."

"You mean you wasted a whole wish on having me over for lunch!"

"I did. And don't make me regret it."

I didn't say anything. She squeezed my arm on our way to the wine store.

I decided to stop by the florist nearby.

"He'll love the flowers."

"I haven't bought flowers in years."

She gave a perfunctory nod.

"They're not just for him," I said.

"I know," she said ever so lightly, almost feigning to overlook what I'd said.

Her father's home was a penthouse over-looking the Tiber. He had heard the elevator coming up and was already waiting at the doorway. Only one of the doors was opened, so that it was difficult to fit in with the dog, the cake, the fish, scallops, and spinach, the two bottles of wine, my duffel bag, her backpack, my bag of persimmons, and the flowers — all seemed to want to thrust their way in at the same time. Her father attempted to relieve her of some of her packages. Instead, she let him have the dog, who knew him and right away began jumping and nuzzling him.

"He loves the dog more than me," she said.

"I don't love the dog more than you. The dog is just easier to love."

"Too subtle for me, Pa," she said, and right away didn't just kiss him but, with her hands still holding the packages, slammed into him with her whole body and kissed him on both cheeks. This, I presumed, was how she loved: fiercely, no holds barred.

Once inside, she dropped the bags, took my jacket, and laid it down neatly on the arm of a sofa in the living room. She also took my bag and placed it on the rug by the sofa then fluffed up a large sofa cushion that seemed to bear the imprint of the head that must have been lying on it moments earlier. On her way to the kitchen, she also straightened two pictures that hung slightly lopsided against the wall, then, opening two French windows that led to the sunbaked roof terrace, complained that the living room was too stuffy on such a beautiful autumn day. In the kitchen, she cut off the bottom tips of the flower stems, found a vase, and set the flowers in it. "I love gladiolas," she said.

"So you must be the guest?" said the father by way of welcome. *"Piacere,"* he added, before reverting to English. We shook hands, hesitated outside the kitchen, and then watched her unwrap the fish, scallops, and spinach. She rummaged through the cabinets, found the spices, and right away used the zapper to light the stove. "We are going to drink some wine, but, Pa, you decide whether you want to drink it now or with the fish."

He mused for a moment. "Both now and with the fish."

"So we're already starting," she said reprovingly.

Pretending to be chastened, the old man said nothing then added an exasperated, "Daughters! What can you do."

Father and daughter spoke the same way. The father then ushered me down a corridor lined with framed pictures of past and present family members, all so formally clothed that I failed to recognize Miranda in any of them. The father was now wearing a colorful ascot, under a very bright striped pink shirt; his blue jeans were creased to a crisp and looked as though they'd been put on minutes earlier. His long white hair was combed back and gave him the telltale look of an aging movie star. But he wore a pair of very old slippers and obviously hadn't had time to shave. His daughter had done well to call to warn him of a visitor. The living room bore the lingering spare elegance of a Danish fad that had gone out of fashion a few decades earlier but was on the verge of being the rage again. The ancient fireplace had been refurbished to fit in with the decor but seemed a defunct remnant of older times in the life of the apartment. The slick white wall displayed a small abstract painting in the style of Nicolas de Staël.

"I like that one," I finally said, trying to make conversation while staring at the view of a beach as seen on a wintry day.

"That one was given to me by my wife years ago. I didn't much like it at the time; but now I realize it's the best thing I own."

The old gentleman, I gathered, had never recovered from his divorce.

"Your wife had good taste," I added, already regretting using the past tense without knowing whether I had strayed into delicate terrain. "And these here," I said, staring at three sepia-toned views of Roman life in the early nineteenth century, "look like Pinellis, don't they?"

"They *are* Pinellis," said the proud father who might have interpreted my comment as a slight.

I'd been tempted to say imitation Pinellis but had caught myself in time.

"I bought them for my wife but she didn't care for them. So they're living with me now. Afterward, who knows. Maybe she'll take them back. She owns a successful gallery in Venice."

"Thanks to you, Pa."

"No, thanks to her and only her."

I tried not to let on that I already knew his wife had left him. But then he must have guessed that Miranda had told me about their marriage. "We're still friends," he added by way of clarifying the situation, "maybe good friends."

"And they," added Miranda, handing each of us a glass of white wine, "have a daughter who is constantly being tugged this way and that between them. I'm giving you less wine than our guest, Pa," she said as she handed him his glass.

"I get it, I get it," replied the father, who rested a palm on his daughter's face in a gesture that spoke all the love in the world.

There was no doubt. She was lovable.

"And you know her how?" he asked, turning to me.

"Actually, I don't know her at all," I said. "We met on the train today, basically less than three hours ago."

The father seemed a bit flummoxed and was awkwardly trying to conceal it. "And so . . ."

"And so nothing, Pa. The poor guy was stood up today by his son and I took such pity on him that I figured I'd cook him a fish, feed him vegetables, maybe throw in some limp *puntarelle* found in your fridge, and send him packing to his hotel where he can't wait to nap and wash his hands of us."

All three of us burst out laughing. "This is how she is. How I managed to put such a prickly urchin on the face of our planet is simply beyond me."

"Best thing you ever did, old man. But you should have seen Sami's face when he realized he was being stood up."

"Did I look that terrible?" I asked.

"She exaggerates, as always," he said.

"He's been pouting ever since I got on the train in Florence."

"I wasn't pouting when you got on in Florence," I said, miming her words.

"Oh, you were so pouting. Even before we started speaking. You didn't even want to make room for my dog when I boarded. Think I didn't notice?"

Once again we all laughed.

"Don't mind her. She's always needling people. Her way of warming up."

Her eyes were glued on me. I liked that she was trying to read my reaction to what her father had just said. Or maybe she was just looking at me, and I liked this too.

When was the last time indeed?

On another wall of the living room hung a series of framed black-and-white photographs of ancient statues, all in striking gradations of black, gray, silver, and white shades. When I looked back at her, both father and daughter caught my glance.

"They're all Miranda's. She took them."

"So this is what you do?"

"This is what I do," she apologized, almost as though saying, *This is all I know how to do.* I regretted how I'd phrased my question.

"Black and whites only. Never color," added her father. "She travels the world — she is going to Cambodia, Vietnam, then Laos and Thailand, which she loves, but she is never happy with her work."

I couldn't resist. "Is anyone happy with their work?"

Miranda threw me a token smile of appreciation for coming to her aid. But her look might as well have meant *Nice try, I don't need rescuing.*

"I had no idea you were a photographer. They're amazing." Then, seeing she wasn't taking the compliment, I added, "They're stunning."

"What did I tell you? Never happy with herself. You can beat your head senseless and she still won't accept a compliment. She has a wonderful offer to work for a large agency —"

"— which she isn't going to accept," she said. "We're not discussing this, Pa."

"Why?" he asked.

"Because Miranda loves Florence," she said.

"We both know that her reason has nothing to do with Florence," said the father, playing up the humor but casting a significant look at his daughter and then at me. "It has to do with her father," he said.

"You're so pigheaded, Pa, that you're convinced you're the center of the universe and that without your blessing every evening star in heaven would snuff out its light and turn to ash," she said.

"Well, this pigheaded man needs a bit more wine before he turns to ashes — which, remember, Mira, is what I specified in my will."

"Not so fast," she said, pushing the open

bottle away from her father's reach.

"What she fails to understand — because of her age, I suppose — is that past a certain point dieting and watching what you eat —"

"— or drink —"

"— serve no purpose and actually cause more harm than good. I think people our age should be allowed to live out the term of their life as they wish. Depriving us of what we want at death's door seems pointless, if not totally evil, don't you think?"

"I think one should always do what one wants," I said, begrudging having been put in the father's camp.

"So speaks the man who knows exactly what he wants, right?" was the ironic broadside coming from the daughter, who hadn't forgotten our conversation on the train.

"How would you know whether I know or don't know what I want?" I shot back.

She didn't answer. She just looked at me and didn't lower her eyes. She wasn't playing my little cat-and-mouse game. "Because I'm the same way," she finally said. She'd seen right through me. And she knew that I knew it. What she may not have guessed was that I loved our playful sparring and her unwillingness to let anything slip by if it came from me. It made me feel unusually important, as if we'd known each other forever and our familiarity in no way diminished our mutual regard. I needed to caress her, to put my arms around her.

"Today's youth is too bright for the likes of us," intervened the father.

"Neither of you knows the first thing about today's youth" came the girl's quick reply. Had I once again been inducted into her father's nursing-home universe sooner than my age allowed?

"Well, then here is one more glass of wine for you, Pa. Because I love you. And more for you as well, Mr. S."

"They don't serve wine where I'm headed, my love, white or red, or even rosé, and frankly I want to down as much of it before they wheel away the gurney. Then I'll sneak a bottle or two under the sheets so that when I finally get to meet His Lordship, I'll say, 'Here, see what goodies I brought you from confounded planet Earth.' "

She did not reply but returned to the kitchen to bring lunch to the dining room. But then she changed her mind and said it was warm enough for the three of us to eat on the veranda. We each took our glasses and our silverware and proceeded to the terrace. Meanwhile, she split open the *branzini* she had broiled in a cast-iron frying pan, removed their bones, and on a different plate came the spinach and old *puntarelle,* over which, once we were seated, she sprinkled oil and freshly grated parmesan.

"So tell us what you do," said the father, turning to me.

I told them that I had just finished working on my book and would soon head back to Liguria, where I lived. I gave them a very hasty outline of my career as a professor of classics and of my current project on the tragic fall of Constantinople in 1453. I told them about my life a bit, about my ex-wife who lives in Milan now, about my son who has a rising career as a pianist, and then told them how much I miss waking up to the sea when I'm away.

The fall of Constantinople interested her father.

"Did the residents know their city was doomed?" asked the father.

"They knew."

"So why didn't more of them flee before it was sacked?"

"Ask the Jews of Germany!"

There was a moment of silence.

"You mean ask my parents and grandparents and most of my aunts and uncles whom I'll soon encounter at the pearly gates?"

I was unable to tell whether Miranda's

father was administering a cold shower after what I'd just said, or whether this was just another not-so-veiled reference to his declining health. Either way, I wasn't scoring points.

"Knowing that the end is near is one thing," I added, trying to navigate a tactful course over the shoals, "but believing it is quite another. Tossing one's entire life overboard to start from scratch in a foreign land may be a heroic act but it is totally reckless. Not many are capable of it. Where do you turn when you feel trapped and caught in a vise, when there is no exit and the house is on fire, and your window is on the fifth floor, so that plunging isn't really an option? There is no other bank. Some people choose to take their own lives. Most, however, prefer to wear blinkers and live off hope. The streets of Constantinople overflowed with the blood of the hopeful once the Turks entered the city and sacked it clean. But I'm interested in the citizens of Constantinople who feared the end and fled, many to Venice."

"Would you have left Berlin if you were living there in, say, 1936?" Miranda asked.

"I don't know. But someone would have had to push me or threaten to leave me behind if I wasn't ready to flee. I am reminded of a violinist who hid in his apartment in the Marais in Paris knowing that the police would come knocking at his door one night. And knock one night they did. He even managed to convince them to let him take his violin with him, and they did. But it was the first thing they took away from him. They killed him, but not in a gas chamber. Instead, in the camps, they beat him to death."

"So your reading this evening will be about Constantinople?" she asked, almost with an incredulous inflection in her voice that made her sound disappointed. It was not clear whether she meant to trivialize my work by asking the sort of question I'd just asked about hers or whether she was filled with admiration, meaning *How wonderful that this should be your life's work!* Which was why I ended up answering with a meek and evasive "That's what I do. But there are days when I am able to see my vocation for what it is: desk work, just desk work. I'm not always proud of this."

"So your life is not spent traipsing through the Aeolian Islands, then settling somewhere like Panarea, swimming at dawn, writing all day, eating from the sea, drinking Sicilian wine at night with someone half your age."

Where was this coming from? And was

she making fun of what every man my age dreams of?

Miranda put down her fork and lit a cigarette. I watched her shake the match with a decisive hand motion before dropping it into an ashtray. How strong and invulnerable she suddenly seemed. She was showing her other side, the one that sizes people up and makes hasty indictments, then shuts them off and never lets them back in except when she weakens, only to hold it against them that she did. Men were like matches: they caught fire and were shaken off and dropped in the first ashtray that came her way. I watched her take in her first puff. Yes, willful and unbending. Smoking with her face turned away from us made her look so distant and heartless. The type who always gets her way. Not exactly the good girl who doesn't like to see people hurt.

I liked watching her smoke. She was beautiful and unreachable, and once again I held myself back from putting my arm around her and letting my lips touch her cheek, her neck, the back of her ear. Could she tell that wanting to hold her both stirred and dismayed me, because I knew there was no room for me in her world? She had invited me for her father's sake.

What made her smoke, though?

Watching her hold her cigarette, I couldn't stop from saying: "As a French poet once said, some people smoke to put nicotine in their veins, others to put a cloud between them and others." But then thinking she'd interpret it as a caustic remark, I quickly turned the tables on myself. "We all have ways of putting up screens to keep life at bay. I use paper."

"Do you think I keep life at bay?" Hers was a frank and hasty query, not a muffled quip asking for trouble.

"I don't know. Perhaps going about one's daily life with all its paltry joys and sorrows is the surest way of keeping true life at bay."

"So there may be no such thing as real life. Only clumsy, ordinary, day-to-day stuff — is this what you think?"

I did not answer.

"I just hope there is more than the day-to-day stuff. But I never found it, maybe because finding it scares me."

I did not reply to this either.

"I never speak to people about this."

"I don't either," I replied.

"I wonder why neither of us does."

This was the girl on the train speaking. Unbending and determined yet totally adrift.

We smiled feebly at each other. Then, sensing that the conversation was taking a strange and awkward turn: "He likes desk work too," she threw in and motioned to her father.

Her father picked up his cue right away.

Great teamwork.

"I do like desk work. I was a good professor. Then about eight years ago, I retired. I help writers and young scholars. They give me their dissertations, and I edit them. It's lonely work but it's lovely and peaceful work. And I always learn so much. I spend long hours this way, sometimes from dawn to midnight. Then late at night I watch television to air out my thoughts a bit."

"His problem is that he forgets to charge them."

"Yes, but they love me and I've grown to love each one, we're always exchanging e-mails. And frankly, I'm not doing it for the money."

"Clearly!" retorted the daughter.

"What are you working on now?" I asked.

"It's a very abstract dissertation about time. It starts with the story, or a parable as he likes to call it, of a young American World War II pilot. He was married to his high school sweetheart in the small town where they grew up. They spent about two weeks together in her parents' home before he shipped off. A year and a day later his plane was shot down over Germany. His young wife received a letter telling her that he was presumed dead. There was no evidence of a crash nor had his remains been found. Not long afterward, his bride enrolled in a college where she eventually met a war veteran who looked like her husband. They were married and had five daughters. She died about a decade ago. A few years after her death, the site of the crash was located and her first husband's dog tag and remains were finally recovered and confirmed through a DNA match with a very distant cousin who had never even heard of the pilot or his wife. Still, the cousin agreed to be tested. The sad part is that by the time the fragments of his body were shipped back to his hometown for proper burial, his wife, both her parents, and the pilot's own parents and all their siblings had died. He had no one left, no family to remember, much less to mourn him. His wife herself had never mentioned him to her daughters. It was as though he had never existed. Except that one day the pilot's wife had taken down an old box of scattered mementos that contained, among other things, the wallet the pilot had left behind. When her daughters asked whose it was, she went to the living room and took down a framed photograph of their father to reveal an old photo tucked right behind it. It was the face of her first husband. They had never known that their mother was married before. She herself never brought him up again.

"To me it proves that life and time are not in sync. It's as if time was all wrong and the wife's life was lived on the wrong bank of the river or, worse yet, on two banks, with neither being the right one. None of us may want to claim to live life in two parallel lanes but all have many lives, one tucked beneath or right alongside the other. Some lives wait their turn because they haven't been lived at all, while others die before they've lived out their time, and some are waiting to be relived because they haven't been lived enough. Basically, we don't know how to think of time, because time doesn't really understand time the way we do, because time couldn't care less what we think of time, because time is just a wobbly, unreliable metaphor for how we think about life. Because ultimately it isn't time that is wrong for us, or we for time. It may be life itself that is wrong."

"Why do you say that?" she asked.

"Because there is death. Because death,

contrary to what everyone tells you, is not part of life. Death is God's great blunder, and sunset and dawn are how he blushes for shame and asks our forgiveness each and every day. I know a thing or two on the subject."

He grew silent. "I love this dissertation," he finally said.

"You've been talking about it for months, Pa. Any idea when he'll be done with it?"

"Well, I think the young man is having a hard time pulling it together, partly because he does not know how to conclude it. Which is why he keeps coming up with more examples. This one is about a married couple who fell into a crevasse in an alpine glacier in Switzerland in 1942 and froze to death. Their bodies were recovered seventy-five years later, along with their shoes, a book, a pocket watch, a backpack, and a bottle. They had seven children, all but two are still alive today. The tragic disappearance of both parents cast a dark, disturbing cloud over their children's lives. Every year, on the anniversary of their parents' disappearance, they would climb the glacier and offer a prayer in their memory. Their youngest daughter was four years old at the time of the disappearance. DNA testing confirmed her parents' identities and provided some type of closure."

"I hate that word: *closure*," said Miranda.

"Maybe because you leave doors open everywhere," snapped the father. He gave her a sidelong, ironic glance meant to say, *You know exactly what I'm referring to.*

She did not respond.

An uncomfortable silence sat between them.

I pretended to ignore it.

"Another tale in the dissertation," continued her father, "touches on an Italian soldier who after being married for twelve days is sent away to the Russian front where he disappears and is listed as missing. In Russia, however, he doesn't die and is rescued by a woman who bears him a child. Many years later, he'll return to Italy to feel as rudderless in a homeland he can't begin to recognize as he does in his adopted Russia, to which he eventually returns for want of a better home. You see, two lives, two lanes, two time zones, with neither being the right one.

"Then there's the tale of a forty-year-old man who one day finally resolves to visit the tombstone of his father who died during the war shortly before his son's birth. What strikes the son as he stands speechless before the dates on the tombstone is that his father died scarcely aged twenty — half the son's current age — and that therefore the son is old enough to be his father's father. Oddly, he can't decide whether he is saddened because his father never got to see him, or because he himself never got to know his father, or because he is standing before the tombstone of someone who feels more like a dead son than a dead father."

Neither of us attempted to lend a moral to this tale.

Said the father, "I find these tales very moving, but I still can't tell why, except that I pick up a suggestion that, despite appearances, living and time are not aligned and have entirely different itineraries. And Miranda is right. Closure, if it exists at all, is either for the afterlife or for those who stay behind. Ultimately, it is the living who'll close the ledger of my life, not I. We pass along our shadow selves and entrust what we've learned, lived, and known to afterpeople. What else can we give those we've loved after we die than pictures of who we were when we were children and had yet to become the fathers they grew up to know. I want those who outlive me to extend my life, not just to remember it."

Catching the two of us silent, her father suddenly exclaimed, "Just bring the cake.

Right now I want to put a cake between me and what awaits me. Maybe He'll appreciate a cake also, don't you think?"

"I bought a smaller cake because I knew you'd finish a larger one by the time I left on Sunday."

"As you can see she wants me to stay alive. What for, I have no idea."

"If not for yourself, then for me, old goon. Besides, don't pretend: I've seen you look at women when we're out walking the dog."

"It's true, I still turn around when I see a beautiful pair of legs. But to tell you the truth, I forget why."

We all laughed.

"I'm sure those visiting nurses will help you remember."

"I may not want to remember what I'm missing."

"I hear there's medication to remind you."

I watched the mock squabbling between father and daughter. She left the table and went into the kitchen to bring more silverware.

"Do you think my health can afford a tiny cup of coffee?" he asked loudly enough for her to hear. "Maybe one for our guest as well?"

"Two hands, Pa, two hands," she pretended to grumble, and moments later brought out the cake and three small dishes, which she left stacked on a stool before going back to the kitchen. We heard her tinker with the coffee maker then bang the residual grinds from this morning's coffee into the sink.

"Not in the sink," he growled.

"Too late," she responded.

The two of us stared at each other and smiled. I couldn't help myself: "She loves you, doesn't she?"

"She does, yes. But she shouldn't. I'm lucky that way. Still, I think it's not good at her age."

"Why?"

"Why? Because I think it's going to be difficult for her. Plus it doesn't take a genius to see I'm standing in the way."

There was nothing to say to this.

We heard her placing the dirty dishes into the sink.

"What were the two of you whispering about?" she said when she stepped back onto the terrace with the coffee.

"Nothing," said the father.

"Don't lie."

"We were talking about you," I said.

"I knew it. He wants grandchildren, right?" she asked.

"I want you to be happy. At least happier

— and with someone you love," threw in the father. "And yes, I want grandchildren. It's just the damned clock. Another one of those instances where life and time don't jibe. And don't tell me you don't understand."

She smiled, meaning she did.

"I'm knocking at death's door, you know."

"Did they answer yet?" she asked.

"Not yet. But I heard the old butler shout a drawn-out 'Com-ing!' and when I knocked again, he groaned, 'I said I was coming, didn't I?' Before they unbolt the door to let me in, could you at least find someone you love."

"I keep telling him there is nobody, but he doesn't believe me," she said, turning to me, as though I were mediating their discussion.

"How could there be nobody?" he replied, turning to me as well. "There is always someone. Every time I call there is someone."

"And yet it is always no one. My father doesn't understand," she said, sensing I was more likely going to side with her. "What these men have to offer I already have. And everything they want they don't deserve, or I may not have in me to give. That's the sad part."

"Strange," I said.

"Why strange?"

She was sitting next to me, away from her father.

"Because I am the exact opposite. I have very little that anyone might want at this point and, as for what *I* want, I wouldn't even know how to spell it out. But all this you know already."

For a moment she just looked at me. "Maybe I do and maybe I don't." Meaning: *I'm not playing your game.* She knew, knew just what I was doing long before I knew I was doing it.

"Maybe you do, and maybe you don't," mimicked her father. "You're so good at finding paradoxes, and once you've fished one out from your bag of easy notions you think you've got your answer. But a paradox is never an answer, it's just a fractured truth, a wisp of meaning without legs. But I am sure our guest did not come to listen to our squabbling. Forgive our father-daughter tiff."

We watched her turn the coffeepot upside down while she covered the spigot with a dish towel to prevent the coffee from spurting. Neither father nor daughter took sugar with coffee, but she suddenly realized that I might want it and, without asking me, rushed to the kitchen to bring the sugar bowl.

I did not usually take sugar, but was touched by her gesture and served myself a teaspoon. Then I wondered why I'd done it when I could so easily have said no.

We drank coffee quietly. After coffee I stood up: "Perhaps it's time I headed to my hotel to review my notes for my reading this evening."

She could not resist. "Do you actually need to review your notes? Haven't you given the same reading several times already?"

"I'm always afraid I'll lose my thread."

"I can't picture you losing your thread, Sami."

"If you only knew what goes on in my head."

"Oh, tell us," she bandied, not without a touch of frisky guile, which surprised me. "I was thinking of coming to your reading today — if I'm invited, that is."

"Of course you're invited, your father too."

"Him?" she asked. "He rarely goes out."

"I do go out," her father shot back. "How would you know what I do when you're not here."

She did not wait to reply but went back into the kitchen and returned with a plate on which she had sliced a persimmon in four. The other two persimmons were not quite ripe yet, she said. Then she left the terrace and came back with a bowl of walnuts. Perhaps it was her way of detaining me a while longer. Her father reached for the bowl and picked one. She did too and found the nutcracker buried underneath the nuts. He did not use the nutcracker, instead cracked a walnut with his hand. "I hate when you do that," she said. "What — this?" And he cracked another one open as well, removed its shell then handed me the edible part. I was mystified. "How did you do that?" I asked. "Simple," he replied. "You don't use your fist, just your index finger, which you place across the seam of both halves, like this, and with the other hand you give it a firm tap. *Voilà!*" he said, offering the contents to his daughter this time. "You try," he said, handing me a new nut. And sure enough, I cracked one open just as he had done.

"You live and learn." He smiled. "I need to get back to my airplane pilot," he added, standing up and pushing his chair back in to the table and leaving the terrace.

"Bathroom," she explained. She sprang up and went straight to the kitchen. I left my seat and followed her, not quite sure whether I was wanted there. So I stood at the entrance and watched her rinse the dishes, one by one, then stack them way too hastily next to the sink before asking me to help her stow them in the dishwasher. She filled the cast-iron frying pan with steaming-hot water and coarse salt and began to scrub it clean, scraping vigorously as if in a fit of bad temper against a piece of burned fish skin that clung to the side of the pan and wouldn't yield to the metal scrubber. Was she upset? When it came to the crystal wine glasses, though, she was gentler, delicate, as though something about their age and rounded shape pleased and soothed her and required watchful deference. So she wasn't angry after all. The rinsing took a few minutes. When she was done, I noticed that the palms of her hands and her fingers had turned a very deep pink, verging on purple. She had beautiful hands. She looked at me while drying them with a small kitchen towel hanging from the refrigerator door handle, the same one she had used to stop the coffee maker from sputtering. She didn't say anything. Then she squeezed a dispenser of hand lotion by the sink and rubbed her hands with the cream.

"You have nice hands."

She didn't respond. All she said after a

pause was "I have nice hands," echoing my words either to deride them or to question my motive for saying them.

"You don't use fingernail polish," I added.

"I know."

Again, I couldn't tell whether she was apologizing for not using polish or telling me to mind my own business. I had meant to suggest she was different from so many women her age who use all manner of color on their fingernails. But then she probably knew this, and didn't need reminding. Lame, lame talk on my part.

When she was done in the kitchen, she walked back into the dining room then headed to the living room to get our jackets. I followed her there, which was when she asked me about my reading tonight. "It's about Photius," I said, "an old Byzantine patriarch who kept a precious catalogue of the books he read called the *Myriobiblion,* meaning 'ten thousand books.' Without his list we'd never have known of the existence of these books — because so many of them have completely disappeared."

Was I boring her? Perhaps she wasn't even listening to me while she riffled through some of the unopened mail sitting on the coffee table.

"So this is what you put between you and

life — ten thousand books?"

I liked her wry humor, especially coming from someone who, despite her very palpable world-weariness on the train, might ultimately prefer cameras, motorbikes, leather jackets, windsurfing, and lean young men who make love at least three times a night. "I put so much stuff between me and life, you have no idea," I said. "But then all this is probably over your head."

"No, it isn't. I know some of it."

"Oh? Like what?"

"Like — do you really want to know?" she asked.

"Of course I want to know."

"Like I don't think you're a very happy man. But then you're a bit like me: some people may be brokenhearted not because they've been hurt but because they've never found someone who mattered enough to hurt them." Then, on second thought, maybe because she felt she had gone too far: "Call it another one of my paradoxes fished out of my overfilled bag of notions. Heartache can be contracted without symptoms. You may not even know you're suffering from it. It reminds me of what they say about a fetus eating its own twin long before being born. There may never be a trace of the missing twin but that child will grow up feeling the absence of his sibling his entire life — the absence of love. Except for my father and what you've said about your son, it seems there may have been very little real love or intimacy in both our lives. But then what do I know."

She hesitated for a very short moment, and, perhaps fearing I'd start countering or taking too seriously what she'd just said, added, "I sense, though, that part of you may not like being told you're not happy." I attempted a polite nod that also meant *I'm just going along with what you're saying and won't argue.* "But the good part is —" she added, then caught herself once again.

"The good part is?" I asked.

"The good part is I don't think you've closed the book or given up looking. For happiness, I mean. I like this about you."

I didn't answer — perhaps my silence was the answer.

"Right," she blurted while handing me my jacket, which I put on. Then, abruptly changing the subject: "Your collar," she said, indicating my jacket.

It was not clear to me what she meant. "Here, let me do it," she said, standing in front of me to straighten my collar. Without giving it another thought, I found myself holding both her hands on the lapels of my jacket against my chest.

I had planned nothing of the sort but simply let myself go and touched her forehead with my palm. I've seldom been this impulsive and to show I didn't mean to cross a line began buttoning my jacket.

"You don't have to go yet," she suddenly said.

"But I should. My notes, my little talk, dead old Photius, the flimsy little screens I put up between me and the real world, they're all waiting, you know."

"This was special. For me, that is."

"This?" I asked, though I couldn't quite bring myself to believe that I knew exactly what she meant. I tried to withdraw but caressed her forehead one last time. Then kissed it. This time I stared at her, she wouldn't look away. And in a gesture that caught me totally by surprise again and seemed to spring from who knows how many years back, I let my fingertip touch her on the chin, softly, the way a grown-up might hold a child's chin between his thumb and forefinger to prevent it from crying, sensing all along, as she did herself, that, if she didn't move, this caress on the chin was probably a prelude to what I did next, when I allowed my finger to travel along her lower lip — back and forth, back and forth. She did not move away but continued to stare at me. Nor could I tell whether I had offended her by touching her forehead this way, or whether, taken aback, she was still mulling over how to react. And still she continued to stare, bold and unbending. I ended up apologizing.

"It's okay," she said, with the start of what appeared to be a suppressed giggle. She was, I was persuaded, overlooking the whole thing and being a grown-up about it. All she did in the end was to turn around sharply and, without saying anything, simply pick up her leather jacket from the sofa. Her gesture was so brusque and so resolute that I was convinced I had upset her.

"I'm coming with you to the lecture hall."

This baffled me. I was sure that she wanted nothing to do with me after what I'd just done.

"Now?"

"Of course now." Then, perhaps to soften her abrupt turn, she added, "Because if I don't keep an eye on you and follow you around town I know I'll never see you again."

"You don't trust me."

"I'm not sure." Then, turning to her father who was seated in the living room now: "Pa, I'm going to hear his talk."

79

He was surprised and probably disappointed that she was leaving so soon. "But you just got here. Weren't you going to read to me?"

"I'll read tomorrow. Promise."

She was in the habit of reading to him from Chateaubriand's *Memoirs*. He used to read Chateaubriand to her when she was in her early teens; now it was her turn, she said.

"Your father isn't very pleased," I said as we were about to leave. She shut the French windows. The room immediately darkened, and the sudden darkness cast a gloomy air that reflected the nearing end of fall and her father's mood.

"He isn't pleased. But it makes no difference. He pretends he's going to work but he takes such long naps these days. In any event, when he naps I usually shop around to replenish his fridge with things he likes. I'll do that tomorrow. The nursing service takes care of the rest. His person will come this afternoon and will also walk the dog, cook, watch TV with him, put him to bed."

When we had gone downstairs and exited the building and were facing the Lungotevere she suddenly stood still and took a deep, deep breath of fresh late-October air.

It surprised me.

"What was that for?" I asked, obviously referring to what had sounded like a mournful sound emanating from her lungs.

"Happens every time I leave. Overwhelming relief. As if I've been choking on bad air inside. One day, soon, I know, I'll miss these visits. I just hope I won't feel guilty or forget why I so badly needed to leave and shut the door behind me."

"Sometimes I wonder if my son doesn't have the same feeling each time he leaves me."

She did not answer. She simply kept walking.

"What I need is a cup of coffee."

"Didn't you just have one?" I asked.

"That was decaf," she said. "I buy decaf coffee for him, which I let him think is regular coffee."

"Is he fooled?"

"Fooled enough. Unless he goes out to get real coffee himself and doesn't tell me. But I doubt it. As I told you, I'm here every weekend. Sometimes, when I have a free day, I'll hop on a train and spend the night here and then head back by late morning."

"Do you like coming home?"

"I used to."

And then I found myself asking something

I'd never have dared ask.

"Love him?"

"Hard to say these days."

"Still, you're an amazing daughter. I've seen it with my own eyes."

She did not reply. A disabused smile that seemed to say *You don't know the half of it* hovered over her features. "I think the love I once had has run its course. What remains is just placebo love, easy to mistake for real love. Aging, sickness, maybe the start of dementia will do this. Taking care of him and worrying for him and calling him all the time when I'm away to make sure he lacks for nothing — all these have worn out everything I had in me to give. You wouldn't call this love. No one would. He wouldn't."

Then, as she'd already done before, she cut herself short: "Girl needs coffee!" Suddenly, she picked up her pace. "I know a nice place nearby."

As we were headed to her café, I asked if she minded making a very short stop across the bridge. "I want to take you somewhere."

She did not ask why or where but simply followed. "Are you sure you have time? You need to drop your bag, wash your hands, review your notes, who knows what else," she said with a perceptible snicker in her voice.

"I have time. Maybe I was exaggerating before."

"You don't say! I knew you were a fibber."

We laughed. Then, out of the blue: "He is very sick, you know. And the worst is, he knows it, even if he doesn't want to talk about it. I still can't tell whether it's because he's too scared to bring it up or just trying not to scare me. We both allege it's to protect the other, but I think we haven't found a way to talk about it and prefer to postpone confronting it until it may be too late. So we keep it very light, and joke about it. 'Did you bring the cake?' 'I brought the cake.' 'Some more wine for me?' 'Yes, but only a drop more, Pa.' In a short while he won't be able to breathe, so if the cancer doesn't kill him, pneumonia will. To say nothing of the morphine he's started taking and which eventually causes other problems we don't need to talk about. I may have to move in with him if none of my siblings will. We all say we'll take turns, but who knows what excuses each will find when the time comes."

On our way we took a slight detour and stopped at my hotel. I said I was going in to drop my bag at the desk. The attendant, who was watching television, said he would have one of the bellhops bring it up to my room. Miranda didn't enter the lobby but took a peek at the little chapel inside the hotel. When I came out I saw her using the toe of her boot to fiddle with a loose cobblestone that seemed to interest her.

"Two minutes and you'll see what I meant to show you," I said, sensing her edginess. I wanted to say something about her father, or at least close the subject with a few comforting words. But I couldn't think of a thing that wasn't a platitude and was glad she had dropped the subject.

"This better be worth it," she said.

"It is to me."

Within a few minutes we approached a building on the corner of the street. I stopped in front of it and stood quiet.

"Don't tell me — vigil!"

She remembered.

"Where?" she asked.

"Upstairs. Third floor, large windows."

"Happy memories?"

"Not especially. I just lived here."

"And?"

"If I come back to my hotel each time I'm in Rome it's because it's just a few steps away from this building," I said, pointing to the windows upstairs that clearly hadn't been cleaned or replaced in decades. "I love to hover here. Then it's as if I'm still upstairs, still reading Ancient Greek, still grading student papers. I learned to cook in this building. I even learned to sew buttons here. Learned to make my own yogurt, my own bread. Learned the I-Ching. Had my first pet because the old French lady downstairs didn't want her cat any longer, and the cat liked me. I envy that young man living upstairs, though he wasn't very happy here. I like to come back later in the evening when it grows dark to watch the apartment. Then if a light goes on at my old windows, my heart just bursts."

"Why?"

"Because part of me probably hasn't given up wanting to turn back the clock. Or hasn't quite accepted that I've moved on — if indeed I did move on. Perhaps all I truly want is to reconnect with the person I used to be and lost track of and simply turned my back on once I moved elsewhere. I may never want to be who I was in those days, but I do want to see him again, just for a minute or so to find out who this person is who hasn't even left the wife he hasn't met yet, and who is still so far from knowing he'll be a father someday. The young man upstairs knows nothing of this, and part of me wants to bring him up-to-date and let him know I'm still alive, that I haven't changed, and that I'm standing outside here right now —"

"— with me," she interrupted. "Maybe we can go upstairs and say hello. I'm dying to meet him."

I couldn't tell whether she was taking the joke to the next level or being oddly serious.

"I'm sure he would have loved nothing more than to open the door and see you waiting on the landing," I said.

"Would you have let me in?" she asked.

"You know the answer!"

She waited for me to add something, perhaps to clarify my meaning. But I didn't.

"Thought so."

"Would *you* have come in?" I finally asked.

She thought for a second.

"No," she replied.

"Why not?"

"I like the older you better."

A sudden silence fell between us.

"Better answer?" she asked, ribbing my arm in a gesture that could easily have meant that even in jest there was earnest and trusting fellowship between us.

"I am much older than you, Miranda," I said.

"Age is what it is. Cool?" she replied

86

almost before I'd finished uttering my sentence.

"Cool." I smiled. I'd never used the word this way before.

"So, have you ever stepped inside the building or gone upstairs?" She was changing the subject.

Figures, I thought.

"No, never."

"Why not?"

"I don't know."

"Did Miss Margutta hurt you that badly?"

"I don't think so. The building has very little to do with her. Other girls came here, though."

"Did you like them?"

"I liked them well enough. I remember one day in particular when I had the flu and had canceled all my classes and lessons. It was one of my happiest days here. I had a fever and no food at home. A girl who was my student heard I was sick and brought me three oranges, stayed awhile, ended up making out with me, then left. A short while later another girl brought me chicken soup, a third dropped by and made hot toddies with so much brandy for the three of us that I think I was the happiest man with a fever. One of those two ended up living with me for a while."

87

"And yet, right now, I'm the one standing with you here. Did that occur to you?"

There was something unusually pinched in her voice, and I couldn't tell why. I thought I was confiding my past, the way we'd been doing since riding the train together. Then I gave a light chuckle that I could tell sounded slightly forced.

"What's so funny?"

"It's not funny, it's just that you weren't even born when I used to live here."

Neither of us asked why the matter had come up.

She took out a small camera from her bag. "I'm going to ask these people to take a picture of the two of us, so you'll know I existed and wasn't reduced to a fleeting memory like that girl with three oranges whose first, last, and middle name you can't for the life of you remember now."

Was all this a frenzy of female vanity? She wasn't the type.

She stopped a couple of American tourists coming out of a store and, handing one of them her camera, asked the blond girl to take a picture of us in front of the building. "Not like this," she said. "Put your arm around me. And give me your other hand. It won't kill you."

She asked the girl to take another picture

for good measure.

After watching the girl snap a few more times, she thanked her and retrieved her camera. "I'll send you the photos soon enough so you won't forget Miranda. Promise?"

I promised.

"Does Miranda care that much?"

"You still don't understand, do you? When was the last time you were with a girl my age who's not exactly ugly and who is desperately trying to tell you something that should have been quite obvious by now?"

I had suspected she was about to say something like this, so why did it give me a start and make me hope I'd misread her?

Say it plainly, Miranda, or say it again.

Wasn't that plain enough?

Then say it again.

The words we'd spoken were sufficiently vague for us not to know what the other meant or what we ourselves meant, yet we both immediately sensed, without knowing why, that we'd seized the other's underlying meaning precisely because it wasn't spoken.

Right then I had a splendid idea. I took out my cell phone and asked if she had anything to do for the next two to three hours.

"I'm free," she replied, "but don't you

have things to do, notes to go over, clothes to hang up, to say nothing of those hands you needed to wash?"

I didn't have time to explain and right away called a friend who was a well-known archaeologist in Rome. When he picked up, I said, "I need a favor, and I need it today."

"I'm very well, and thank you for asking," he replied with his usual humor. "So how can I help?"

"I need permission for two to visit Villa Albani."

He hesitated a moment. "Is she beautiful?" he asked.

"Totally."

"I've never been inside Villa Albani," she said. "They never let anyone in."

"You'll see." Then, as I waited for his call back: "Cardinal Albani built his villa in the eighteenth century and amassed a huge collection of Roman statues under the care of Winckelmann, and I want you to see them."

"Why?"

"Well, you fed me fish and walnuts, and you love statues, so I'll show you the most beautiful bas-relief you'll see in your life. It's of Antinoüs, Emperor Hadrian's lover. Then I'll show you my favorite — a statue of Apollo killing a lizard, attributed to Praxiteles, possibly the greatest sculptor of all time."

"And my cup of coffee?"

"We have plenty of time."

My phone rang. Could we be at the villa within the hour? The visit would last no longer than an hour because the custodian needed to leave early. "It's Friday," explained my friend.

We found a cab waiting right off the bridge and in seconds were racing to the villa. In the cab she turned to me. "What made you want to do this?"

"My way of showing that I am happy I listened to you."

"Despite your grumbling?"

"Despite my grumbling."

She said nothing, looked out for a short moment, then turned back to me.

"You surprise me."

"Why?"

"I didn't expect you to be the kind who jumps on impulse from one thing to the next."

"Why?"

"Because there's something so thoughtful, calming, even-tempered about you."

"You mean dull."

"Not at all. People trust you and want to open up to you, maybe because they like who they are when they're with you — like right now in this cab."

I reached out, held her hand, then let it go.

We arrived in less than twenty minutes. The custodian had been warned of our arrival and was waiting outside the small gate with his arms crossed, almost peremptory and hostile. He eventually recognized me and his attitude, mistrusting at first, changed to one of guarded respect. We entered the villa itself and headed upstairs and proceeded through a series of chambers until we stood facing the statue of Apollo. "It's called the Sauroktonos, killer of snakes. We'll walk through the gallery and, if there's time, see the Etruscan panels."

She stared at it, said she was sure she'd seen a copy of the statue before, but not that one.

We rushed through the rest until we got to the Antinoüs. She couldn't have been more struck by its beauty. "It's amazing."

"What did I tell you?"

"Sono senza parole," she said. I'm without words right now.

Both of us were. She put her arm around me, stared for a while, then rubbed my back once. Then we moved away.

A short while later I turned to her and,

pointing to a small bust of a hunchback, whispered in her ear that she could sneak a few pictures with her tiny camera if I managed to distract the guard, as no one was allowed to take photos. I remembered that he'd once opened up to me about his sick mother, so taking him aside, I asked how his mother had handled her operation. The question was meant to suggest *delicatezza* as I was asking it sotto voce allegedly so Miranda wouldn't hear. He appreciated my discretion and explained that *purtroppo era mancata.* I gave him my sympathies and to detain him a while longer and make certain that his back was turned to Miranda, explained that my mother too had died. "We're given one only," he said. We nodded and commiserated.

Back to the Sauroktonos for one last look, I explained that the same statue was in the Louvre and in the Vatican Museums, but this and the one in Cleveland were the only ones in bronze. "But this one is not life-size," said the guard. "Cleveland's, I'm told, is more beautiful."

"It is," I said.

Then he encouraged us to walk through the Italian garden that led to another gallery filled with statues. At one point in the garden, we turned around to take in the façade and magnificent arcade of the large neoclassical palazzo, once deemed the most beautiful of its day.

"I think we won't have time to see the Etruscan panels," he added, "but *in compenso* maybe the signorina might wish to take a few pictures of these statues, seeing," he added with a mischievous, smug smile, "she likes taking pictures." We all smiled at one another. He led us through the garden then to the exit gates, pointing to what he claimed were the seven oldest pine trees in Rome. As he pressed the button to open the electric gate, an elderly gentleman standing on the sidewalk stared at us and couldn't help saying to the guard, "My family has lived in Rome for seven generations, yet never once has any of us been allowed into this villa." The guard put on his peremptory gaze again and told him it was *vietato,* forbidden, to let anyone in. The gate closed behind us.

Before hailing a cab, she said she wanted to take another picture of me by the gate.

"Why?" I asked.

"No reason."

Then, seeing I looked mopey, "Could you kill that frown?" she said. But then, reacting to my smile: "And not a fake Hollywood smile — please!"

She snapped a few photos. But she wasn't happy. "Why did you frown?"

I didn't know why I had, I said. But I did know.

"Yet this morning you're the one who accused *me* of being glum!"

We laughed.

She did not seem to expect a comment from me. Nor did I push her to explain. But as she kept clicking away, a troubling awareness began to creep up on me: someday, this would be a vigil too and it would be called *Kill the frown!* There was something warm, lambent, and intimate each time she elbowed me this way. She reminded me of someone who storms into your life, just as she'd done in her father's living room, and right away fluffs your pillows, tears open the windows, straightens two old paintings you've stopped seeing though they'd never budged from your mantelpiece for years, and with a deft foot flattens the ripples on an ancient rug, only to remind you, once she's added flowers to a vase that's been standing empty for ever so long that, in case you were still struggling to downplay her presence, you wouldn't dare ask for more than a week, a day, an hour of this. How close had I come to someone so real, I thought. How close.

Was it too late?

Am I too late?

"Stop thinking," she said.

I reached out and held her hand.

In the swanky, crowded Caffè Trilussa that she liked we found a small, rickety square table and sat facing each other. Behind her stood one of those outdoor heaters going full blast. She liked the heat, she said, adding how strange it was that just a few hours earlier it had been warm enough to eat on her father's terrace. Now she wanted something warm to drink. When the waiter came, she ordered two double Americanos.

What's an Americano, I was going to ask, but caught myself and decided not to. It took me a few moments to realize why I hadn't asked.

"An Americano is when they add hot water to a cup of espresso. A double Americano is hot water and two shots of espresso."

She lowered her gaze and looked down at the table trying to stifle a smile.

"How could you tell I didn't know what an Americano was?"

"I just knew."

"I just knew," I repeated.

I loved this. I think we both did.

"Is it because your father wouldn't know,

so you figured I wouldn't either?"

"Wrong!" she said, immediately guessing why I'd asked. "That's not why at all, mister. I already told you."

"Then why?"

Suddenly, the jeering smile vanished from her face.

"I know you, Sami, that's why. I look at you now, and it's as if I've known you forever. And here's one more thing, since we're on the subject and I'm the one doing all the talking."

Where was she headed with this?

"I don't want to stop knowing you. So there's the long and the short of it."

I looked at her once again, still uncertain what all this added up to. *Just don't make me hope, Miranda, don't.* I didn't even want to raise the subject with her because that would be hoping too.

The waiter brought us two cups.

"An Americano," she said, adopting the playful tone of moments before, "is for people who want an espresso but like American coffee. Or it's for people who just want an espresso that lasts a long time —"

"Go back to what you were saying before," I interrupted.

"What was I saying?" She was teasing. "That I've known you forever? Or that I don't want to stop knowing you? The two go together."

When had all of this happened? In the train, in the taxi, in her father's apartment, the kitchen, the living room, outside Villa Albani, when we spoke of Miss Margutta, or passed by my old home? Why did I feel she kept throwing me off course when part of me knew she wasn't doing it at all?

She must have known what I felt; it should have been clear from the very start to a child of six. But in Miranda, when? A few whimsical minutes ago that could so easily wilt no sooner than I'd mistake them for real? And then the thought struck again. Years ago, in a building not three blocks from here, I was reading Byzantine scholiasts, lost in the world of pre-Islamic Constantinople, yet the sperm cell from her pa's gonads that would become Miranda hadn't even been released. I stared at her. She gave a forced, diffident smile that didn't sit with the jaunty, willful, unbending girl who knew all about Americanos. I could have asked her, *What's the matter?* But I resisted. All she did at the end of an uncomfortable pause when neither of us said anything was to shake her head slightly, as though disagreeing with herself and dismissing a silly notion that she knew better than to confide. I'd already seen her do this the moment she sat across from me on the train. Now she looked down at her coffee cup. Her silence unsettled me.

We were staring at each other, and yet neither of us was saying anything. I knew that if I uttered another word I would break the spell, so we sat there, silent and staring, silent and staring, as if she too did not want to lift the spell. I wanted to ask, *What are you doing in my life? And do people so young and beautiful really exist? Are they even real outside films and magazines?*

And suddenly the Ancient Greek verb ὀψίζω, *opsizo,* raced through my mind. I tried to resist telling her, but then I couldn't help myself. I explained that *opsizo* meant to arrive too late to the feast, or just before last call, or to feast today with the weight of all the wasted yesteryears.

"And your point is?"

"Nothing."

"Exactly."

She nudged me, meaning *Don't go there!* Then she pointed to a woman who'd been sitting by herself at another table. "She keeps staring at you." I didn't believe her but I liked the idea. Another person was struggling with the crossword puzzle. "She's not making good progress," said Miranda. "Maybe I should help her with a hint; I finished mine this morning at the station. And by the way, that other one looked at you again, four o'clock, to your right."

"Why is it that I never notice these things?"

"Maybe because you're not a present-tense kind of person. This, for instance, is the present tense," she said, reaching over and kissing me on the lips. It was not a full kiss, but it lingered and she let her tongue touch my lips. "And you smell good," she said.

Okay, I am fourteen now, I thought.

Later, while giving my audience a harrowing description of the sack of Constantinople by the Ottomans, I recalled how she'd held my hand as we threaded our way through the narrow streets of Trastevere, as though she were scared to lose me in the crowd, when it was I who feared she might any moment be the one to drop my hand and slink away. And I thought of how she burrowed into my arms when I finally held her when we'd stepped outside Caffè Trilussa and how she'd placed both fists against my chest as though struggling against my hug and pushing me away when I realized it was just her way of folding into me before I let myself go and kissed her. I hadn't kissed a woman in so very long, and certainly not with so much passion and I was about to tell her so, when she simply said, "Keep holding me, just keep holding me, Sami, and kiss me."

What a woman.

And as I was still going on and on about the unimaginable loss of so many works in Photius's catalogue of books, I was saving the best of our duet for last. "I know one thing," I'd told her. "What?" "Come stay with me. I have a house by the sea." The thought had just come to me as we were talking and I had sprung it on her without even thinking. I'd never said anything remotely like this in my life. Her reply was more startling and disarming than what I'd just said.

"My friends would find this hysterical and think, Miranda's lost her mind."

"I know. But do you want to?"

"Yes."

Then, in what first appeared to be a second thought on her part: "For how long?" And this too I'd never said before but I knew I meant every word: "For as long as you want, for as long as you live." We laughed. We laughed because neither of us believed the other was serious. I laughed because I knew I was.

And then, without losing my train of thought as I kept addressing the audience about the books that mankind had lost forever, I imagined how she'd look with her face all flushed and, with her bare knees parted, how she'd guide me with the same hand I'd held and that one day soon would taste of brine after swimming in the Tyrrhenian Sea minutes before noon every day.

"This is what we'll do," she said once we were heading up Via Garibaldi. "I'll sit in the back somewhere invisible in the audience and I'll just wait, because I'm sure everyone is going to want to talk to you and ask questions about the reading and your other books, and then we'll sneak off and go for dinner somewhere where they serve good wine, because I want very good wine tonight. Then, after dinner, we'll have a nightcap in a bar I know and you'll tell me everything you already told me about everyone in your life and I'll tell you all you wish to know about me and after that I'll walk you back to your hotel or you can walk me back to my dad's, and I might as well tell you now: I'm terrible the first time."

I admired her for saying something most people won't even discuss before the fact.

"Who isn't terrible the first time?"

"How would you know?"

It made the two of us laugh.

"Why are you terrible?" I asked.

"It takes me a while to get used to someone. Maybe nerves, though I don't feel nervous with you — which makes me plenty nervous in itself. I don't want to be nervous."

"Miranda," I said, as we stopped by the tiny Tempietto of San Pietro in Montorio and I held her as we looked at Bramante's masterpiece. "Is any of this real?"

"You tell me, but tell me now. I don't need proof, and neither do you. But I don't want surprises. And I don't want to get hurt."

"Cool," I heard myself say. It made the two of us laugh.

"Then we're good."

When we arrived at the hall, we were interrupted by the director, who wanted to escort me to a makeshift greenroom. We separated hastily. She motioned she was going to wait outside after my reading.

It happened right after I was putting my pages back into my slim leather folder. I shook hands with my host, then with another professor, and with all the eager specialists, fellows, and students who had come up to the podium afterward. But my behavior was meant to convey haste. One of the older fellows, who sensed I was eager to leave, made a move to escort me away but then ended up cornering me at the door to ask whether I might read the galleys of his forthcoming book on Alcibiades and the Sicilian expedition. Our topics were closer than they might seem, he said. "You have no idea how similar our interests are," he went on. Would I introduce him to my editor? Of course, I said. No sooner was I free of him than I was buttonholed by an elderly lady who said she had read all my books. She had, as I counted the minutes and inches between us, a terrible habit of spitting as she spoke.

Finally, I was able to leave the auditorium and reach Miranda where I knew she was waiting. But when I looked she wasn't there.

I hurried downstairs by the main stairwell but she was not in the lobby either, so I climbed the stairs to the second floor again and walked around the concourse circling the auditorium. No one. Neither of us had thought of exchanging cell phone numbers. Why on earth hadn't we? I opened the heavy metal door to the auditorium. There were still a few students chatting by the doorway, all clearly about to leave, while two janitors were already picking up empty paper cups and litter in the aisles. Next to the door stood another janitor with a giant key chain who seemed about to lose patience as he waited for everyone, including the dean, to clear out so his staff could go about their business.

Back on the concourse and seeing no one was watching, I even opened the door to the women's bathroom and called out her name. No one answered. Had she gone to the bathroom in the basement? The basement was entirely dark.

Once I walked out of the building, I caught the dark outline of a group of people gathered outside the corner café. She was bound to be inside. She wasn't. I wanted to blame the fussy fellow and the foppish old lady spittle-prattling me to death. I had told Miranda that I'd be out within ten minutes max. Had I totally miscalculated? Or was it my fault because I couldn't say no to people asking for an autograph?

I saw the same foreman with the large key ring shuffling out of the building and locking one of the exit doors. I was tempted to ask him if he'd seen a young lady looking for her — who should I say I was? — her father?

Should I check at her father's?

And then it finally hit me. Why hadn't I thought of it sooner? She had disappeared.

Changed her mind, bolted. No different from how she confessed sloughing off people without so much as a sign or a warning. Pfffff, and in her own words, she was out!

The whole thing was a fantasy. I'd made it all up. The train, the fish, the lunch, Bramante's Tempietto, the young airplane pilot, the Swiss parents who fell into a crevasse and weren't heard from again until their daughter was older than they'd ever been, the Greeks who'd foreseen the end of Byzantium and fled to Venice and passed on their Greek to generations to come until no one recalled why a few Greek words had crept into their Venetian — all, all of it unreal. *What an idiot!*

The word sprang to my lips and I heard it from my own mouth. It made me want to laugh. I repeated the word. *Ee-jit.* A bit less funny the second time, still less the third. *What were you thinking?* I could just hear my son saying this when I saw him tomorrow and told him about the girl on the train called Miranda who took me to her father's house and made me want things I'd thought were forever gone from my life.

It was quite dark and I caught myself taking the only path I knew down the Gianicolo and eventually passed by my old building, as if it could reset my bearings and bring me back to earth and remind me who I was. There it stood, sooner than I'd expected, aged and tilting against time, like me and all my drivel vigils. This too made me want to laugh. All those years and you still haven't learned a thing, have you, still hoping she'd show up at your door, saying, *Here I am, all yours.*

Ee-jit. Of course she had bolted.

In two years when they invite me again, I'll pass by this spot and laugh at the person I hoped to be, at the life I dreamed of sharing in my house by the beach. *Only vigils, now.* For a moment I'd meant to tell her, *I'm ready to drop everything. I don't care where, when, or for how long you want. I don't care.*

Here, tonight, I became a minus.

I couldn't even feel anger, at her or myself. Instead it was resentment. Resentment not that she had lied, or played me, or let her fantasies run wild for a moment and stir mine, all the better to dash them, but that she had changed her mind — and who could blame her for that? Resentment because I had given her my trust, and there was no taking trust back. She had crushed it and shot it down the chute without giving my trust or me another thought. I wanted back the me I'd been this morning on the train, and I wanted the whole thing erased — none of it had happened. *Ee-jit. Of course it hadn't.*

After this, I kept thinking, we'll turn off the lights, lock the doors, pull down the blinds, and learn never to hope again. Not in this lifetime.

I did not need to cross the bridge. All I did was look up at the last floor of her father's building to see that all the lights were out. *Not home. Figures.*

She knew I'd come and had stayed out on purpose. So I walked back to my hotel. Before entering I realized that my original plan wasn't so bad after all. Get a bite to eat, catch a movie, have a drink, go to bed — and leave Rome after seeing my son. And then put it behind me.

But still! Sad how things had turned out.

I was about to tell the hotel clerk that I wanted them to wake me up at seven thirty a.m. when I spotted Miranda. She was sitting at one of the many coffee tables along the long corridor beyond the hotel lobby, leafing through a magazine. "I thought for a second that you'd decided to bolt after all. So I waited. I'm never letting you out of my sight again."

Instead of speaking, I merely hugged her.

"I thought . . ."

"Idiot!" she said. Then, softening her tone: "But you found me."

I handed the clerk my leather folder and we walked out.

"You promised me dinner."

"Dinner it is."

"Where do you normally go after a reading here?"

I told her the name. She knew the place. They gave us a quiet corner table, and the wine was plentiful, not the best, but we managed to empty a bottle. Later, we passed my old building again. When I looked up, I saw a light on in the third floor. "Hurts?" she asked. "No." "Why not?" I gave her a *you're fishing* look and smiled.

She took out her large camera and began taking quick shots of the building, of my window where the light was. "What do you think he's doing upstairs?"

"Oh, I don't know." But what I thought was: The young man upstairs is waiting, still waiting. How would he have known years ago that you weren't born yet? On winter nights when I cooked upstairs and would occasionally look out my kitchen window, I was waiting, but it was always someone else who knocked at my door. In seminars, when I'd light up a cigarette — and in those years you could — I waited for you to open the door. In a crowded movie theater, in bars with friends, everywhere, I waited. But I couldn't find you, and you never came. I kept hoping to run into you at so many parties, and sometimes I almost thought I had, but it was never you, you were two years old at the time, and while we're ordering a second round of drinks, your parents are reading you a second bedtime story. And always, as ever, the clock is ticking. In the end, I stopped waiting, because I stopped believing that you'd stray into my life because I no longer trusted you existed. Everything else happened in my life — Miss Margutta, my marriage, Italy, my son, my career, my books — but you didn't. I stopped waiting and learned to live without you.

"What was it that you so desperately wanted in those years?"

"Someone who knew me inside out, who was me in you, basically."

"Let's go inside," she said.

For a moment I thought she meant for us to go upstairs and had a terrible vision of disturbing the current tenant. "Let's not."

"I meant inside the lobby."

She did not wait for my reply but opened the large glass door.

I told her that the lobby still smelled as it always had, almost three decades later, a blend of cat litter, mold, and rotting wood paneling.

"Lobbies never age, didn't you know? Stand there," she said, taking more pictures of me in the lobby. As she kept backing up to fit me in the frame, I felt drawn closer to her.

"You moved."

"Miranda," I finally said. "Nothing like this has ever happened to me. And here is what's so scary."

"What this time?"

"I could have missed our train and never known how dead I've been all my life."

"You're just scared."

"Of what, though?"

"That tomorrow this could blow away. It doesn't have to."

And this time, standing in my old lobby whose smell I knew so well, I wanted to tell her how strange it was to be back here and feel that the years in between were simply a no-man's-land of such small, trivial joys, all of it like rust over my life. *I want to scrape off the rust, start here again, and redo the whole thing with you.*

I did not speak my sentence but stood there.

"What is it?" she asked.

I shook my head. Instead, I quoted words by Goethe: "Everything in my life was merely prologue until now, merely delay, merely pastime, merely waste of time until I came to know you."

She lowered her camera as I kept drawing closer. She knew I was going to kiss her, so she slammed her back to the wall. "Kiss me, just kiss me." I cupped her cheeks in both hands and brought my lips to hers, kissed her gently on the lips, then with all the passion and desire I'd been trying to suppress since lunch, since watching her rinse the dishes, since she leaned over while talking to the fish vendor and made me want to kiss her face, her neck, her shoulders. I thought I was going to remember a girl I'd kissed years before in that very same lobby, but all I remembered was the imperishable stench of the moldy mat lingering there. *Lobbies never age. We don't either,* I thought. *Oh, but we do age. We don't grow up.*

"I knew it would be like this," she said.

"How like this?"

"I don't know." Then, a moment later, "Again," she said. And because I wasn't reacting fast enough, she pulled me toward her and, without holding back, kissed me with her mouth so open that I felt dazed.

Her hands were pressed against both sides of my face until totally unexpectedly one of her hands cupped where I was getting hard. "I knew he'd like me."

We left my old building, we walked down the main stretch of street vendors who never seem to go to sleep. There was ferment in the alleys and I liked the festive crowds and the overbrimming restaurants and *enoteche,* each with its infrared heat lamps. "I love these narrow alleys by night," she said. "I grew up here."

I held her in both arms and kissed her again. I loved knowing about her life. I told her I wanted to know everything.

"Same here," she said. Then, a moment later, "But there are things you may not want to know — about me, that is," she added. The words she'd just spoken muffled the joy and warmth of the moment. What was she saying? "I shouldn't tell you but I must tell you something I've never ever told anyone because I never met the one person who wants me as I am or, rather, as I've become. And I want you to know it soon, because I'll be forced to hide it, even from you, if I don't let it out now. After this secret, I have nothing to hide. Don't you have a secret like that, a secret that is so burdensome that it becomes a wall that can't be taken down? I want mine down before we make love," she said.

"Of course I have a secret. We all do," I said. "Each of us is like a moon that shows only a few facets to earth, but never its full sphere. Most of us never meet those who'll understand our full rounded self. I show people only that sliver of me I think they'll grasp. I show others other slices. But there's always a facet of darkness I keep to myself."

"I want to know that facet of darkness, tell it to me now. You first, because mine is far worse than anything you'll say."

Perhaps it helped that it was dark when we talked, and as we neared the Basilica of Santa Maria in Trastevere, I told her about Miss Margutta. "You see, our first and only time was in a shabby, cheap hotel in London. We undressed as soon as the landlord showed us to our room. It was late afternoon. We embraced, kissed, embraced again, and were trying too hard, but we persisted, thinking that if desire was giving us the slip, it had done so momentarily and would soon return. But it did not. I was young and vigorous, so I was as baffled as she was. She tried many things but they felt wrong, and I tried too, but I was not arousing her either. Something was off, and though we discussed what it might be, neither could tell the cause. By evening we put our clothes back on and ambled about the streets of Bloomsbury like two lost souls, both pretending we were hungry and were looking for a place where we might find a bite. Instead we drank a lot. When we returned to our room, nothing had changed between us. We did succeed eventually, but it was sex by mutual persistence, not desire, and to top everything, in the moment of alleged ecstasy, I ended up calling her by the name of the woman I was seeing at the time. I'm sure that each of us was relieved to find ourselves back in our respective homes in Rome two days later. She tried very, very hard to stay friends but I avoided her, cold-bloodedly, perhaps because I couldn't face how I'd let her down, or perhaps because I knew I'd sullied my friendship with both her and the man who would become her husband. Years later, when she was very sick and clearly dying, she tried a few times to get in touch with me, but I ducked her and never replied. I'll never, ever forget that."

She listened but said nothing.

"Would you like a gelato?" I asked.

"Would love one."

We entered an ice cream shop. She ordered grapefruit and I pistachio. It was clear she wanted to ask more about what I'd told her but I wanted to hear her tale. "Your turn," I said.

"Promise not to hate me afterward?"

"I'll never hate you."

As we walked out of the ice cream parlor, she said she just loved this, the way the day had turned out, the way we'd met, the reading, dinner, drinks, her father, and now this. "It happened when I was fifteen," she started. "My brother, who was two years older, had a friend over one afternoon, and they were watching TV in his bedroom. I joined them in my typically intrusive-younger-sister way, sat on the bed with them as often happened when I didn't want to be alone in the living room, and we were watching peacefully when my brother put his arm around my shoulder as he sometimes did. But then the other boy did the same. Gradually, the boy's hand moved from my shoulder to under my shirt, and my brother, probably feeling this was still innocent groping that was bound to end the moment I said something, touched my breasts more as a prank than anything else, or perhaps to highlight that there was nothing unusual or shocking in what we were doing. But I didn't object and neither of them was stopping. Then the friend unzipped his pants, and it would still have been little more than naughty horseplay except that my brother, who probably didn't want to be upstaged, did the same. I acted as if the whole thing was natural and then took it a step further and asked the two of them to lie next to me, all three of us huddled together, still watching TV. I trusted my brother and felt safe and knew he would never let this go the distance, except that I let the friend remove my jeans. The friend did not hesitate, and was right away on top of me. He was done in seconds. But now comes the part I'll never live down. It seemed such a silly game that I told my brother it was his turn, and even shamed him for hesitating, which was when I realized — and not before — that the whole thing with his friend was simply a ruse on my part, because I wanted my brother, and I wanted him to make love to me, not just fuck me, because it would have been the most natural thing between us, and perhaps this is what lovemaking is. Even his friend urged him on. *I'd rather not, she's my sister* — I'll never forget his words. He stood up, pulled up his jeans, and lay back down on the bed and continued watching TV. Ever since, my brother will never be alone in the same room with me, and when there's company and we have to sit on the same sofa, he'll make sure to sit at the other end. We have never spoken about this, and to this day I know it stands between us when we kiss hello or hug goodbye, which we avoid whenever possible. I know he's never forgiven himself or me. But it is I who've never forgiven *him.* I was offering him everything I was, because I worshipped my older brother.

"Shocked? Disgusted?"

"No."

She threw away what was left of her ice cream. "I hate the cone part," she said.

Then, changing topics as we were nearing the hotel, she said, "This is not about tonight only."

"Not for me either."

"Just saying," she said. "I have to make a phone call. Don't you?"

I shook my head. "What will you tell him?"

"Who, my father? He's long asleep."

"Your boyfriend!"

"I don't know, it doesn't matter. Is there absolutely no one you need to call?"

I looked at her. "Hasn't been in a long time."

"Just making sure."

"Let's go to my hotel."

She finished her phone call in less than

thirty seconds. "Hasty and perfunctory," I remarked.

"Just like his sex. He said he wasn't surprised. He shouldn't be. That was it. I told him, *No discussion.*"

I liked *No discussion.* One day she'd use *No discussion* with me as well.

As soon as we entered my hotel room, I caught sight of my duffel bag sitting on the luggage rack by a narrow desk. There was only one chair in the room. I remembered packing my bag very early that morning in what suddenly seemed an entirely other lifetime. I remembered its spot near the sofa in her father's home. The bellhop must have brought it up sometime in the afternoon and left it here. A quick look around told me the room was much smaller, even if I always ask for this one. So I apologized to Miranda and said that I liked this room every time I was in Rome because of the balcony. "It's literally seven times the size of the room. The view of Rome is amazing." So I opened the shutters and stepped out onto the balcony. She followed. It was nippy outside, but the view was like her father's, stunning. All the domes of the Roman churches were aglow and had come into view. But the room still felt smaller than I remembered, and there was hardly any space to walk around the large bed. There wasn't even enough light in the room. Yet nothing bothered me. I loved it this way. I threw a sidelong glance at her; nothing seemed to bother her.

I wanted to hold her, then I came up with a singular idea. I was not going to undress just yet. Nor was I going to tear her clothes off the way they do in the movies.

"I want to see you naked, I just want to see. Take off the T-shirt, the shirt, the jeans, the undies, the hiking boots."

"Even the hiking boots and the socks?" she quipped. But she listened, offered no resistance, and proceeded to undress, until she was all naked, standing barefoot on the threadbare carpet that must have been at least twenty years old.

"You like?" she asked.

Since our room faced the courtyard and was exposed to all the other rooms in the hotel I was worried that the other guests might see. But then, *Let them.* She didn't care either. And placing both hands behind the nape of her neck, she assumed a pose that showed off her breasts. They were not big but they were firm.

"Now it's your turn."

I hesitated.

"I don't want shame, I don't want secrets.

Everything is out tonight. No shower, no brushing of teeth, no mouthwash, no deodorant, no anything. I've told you my deepest secret, and you've told me yours. By the time we're done, there mustn't be a living wedge between us, or between us and the world, because I want the world to know us for who we are together. Otherwise there's no point, and I might as well go back to my daddy now."

"Don't go back to your daddy."

"I won't go back to my daddy," she said as the two of us smiled and then laughed. I tendered my left wrist to her, and she began helping remove my cuff links. I hadn't asked her to do this, but she had guessed. I had a feeling she'd done it with other men. I didn't mind.

When I was totally naked, I approached her and for the first time felt her skin, her entire body against mine.

This is what I've always wanted. This and you. Then, because she saw me hesitate, she took my right hand and placed it between her legs, saying, "It's yours, I told you, I don't want the shadow of anything between us, and no half measures. I make no promises, but I'll go all the way with you. Tell me you'll do the same, tell me now, and don't take your hand off. If you're not ready to go all the way —"

"— you'll go back to Daddy. I know, I know."

Talking like this aroused me.

"Now just look at the lighthouse," she said.

I liked her name for it.

I removed the duffel bag from the luggage rack, sat on the rack, and no sooner did I sit down, than she came and sat on my lap and slowly allowed me to penetrate her. "Better now?" she said as we held each other in a very tight embrace. "I'll tell you anything you want to know, anything. Don't move, though." And so saying she squeezed me, which made me pull her even closer. She was teasing me and, holding my head and staring straight at me as she'd done in the coffee shop, finally said, "Just so you know, I have never in all my years been so close to anyone. Have you?"

"Not ever."

"Such a liar," and she squeezed me again.

"You do this once more," I said, "and I won't focus on anything you say."

"What, this?"

"I warned you."

"She was just saying hello."

But unable to hold ourselves back, we began making love in earnest, eventually finding it more comfortable on the bed. "This is all I have, this is all I am," she said.

Later, as we continued to make love, I caressed her face and smiled at her. "I'm holding back," I said. "Me too." She smiled and after touching herself, brought her damp hand to my face, to my cheek and my forehead: "I want you to smell of me." And she touched my lips, my tongue, my eyelids, and I kissed her deep in the mouth, which was a signal we both understood, for it was, from time immemorial, the gift of one human to another human.

"Where did they invent you?" I said when we were resting. What I meant to say was I didn't know what life was before this. So I quoted Goethe again.

"I hope you enjoyed the show," she told the window when a bit later she looked outside and saw that the shutters had stayed open. I shrugged my shoulders. Neither of us cared.

I was about to move.

"Don't go yet. I want us to stay like this." She looked to her left. Neither of us had noticed that a streetlight was shining red and green into our room. "Film noirish," I said.

"Yes, except that I don't want this to turn into one of those Hollywood films where the sobered professor returns meek and chastened to the life he left behind and all he shared with the anonymous lady on the train was a shallow little quiver that couldn't even pass for a heartthrob."

"Never!"

But she looked upset and I thought there were tears welling in her eyes. "Everything I have is yours. Not much, I know," she said. I let a palm rub the tears down from the side of her face.

"Everything you have I've never had. What more is there to want? The question should be: Why am I what you want, when you can do so much better? Children, for instance?"

"Well, that's a no-brainer. I do want a child. But I want it from you and no one else — even if we never see each other after this weekend or after the beach house, or whatever. I think I must have definitely known outside Villa Albani — maybe even before."

"When?"

"Right after you almost kissed me but held back."

"I held back?"

"Did you ever!"

The thought of a child flooded over. "I want your child too. And I want it now." Then I caught myself. "But I shouldn't presume."

"Presume, for God's sake!"

"I'm selfish enough to take everything you're offering."

"Can you do crazy then?" she asked. "Because I can."

"What do you mean by *crazy*?"

"To do in this lifetime everything you couldn't do in your humdrum, day-to-day, sterile, other life? Do you want to do it with me — now?"

"Yes. But can you actually drop everything — your dad, your work?" I asked, almost aware that I sounded like someone looking for excuses to put off making a decision.

"I have my two cameras. It's really all I need. The rest I'll buy anywhere."

She asked if I was sleepy. I wasn't. Did I want to take a short walk? Love to, I said. Via Giulia when it's empty is a dreamland. "There's a wine bar to the right at the very end."

"Shower?" I asked.

"Don't you dare!" she said.

We got dressed quickly. She was wearing what she'd worn on the train. I had brought a pair of chinos that I was only too happy to put on.

Outside the hotel the street was almost deserted.

"I love phantom Rome when it's empty and looks like this."

"Remind you of anything?"

"Not really. You?"

"No. And I don't want it to."

We were holding hands.

"What do you want your new life to be?"

I didn't know what to say. "I want it to be with you. If those we know won't have us the way we are, let's get rid of them. I want to read every book you've read, hear the music you love, go back to the places you know and see the world with your eyes, learn everything you cherish, start life with you. When you go to Thailand, I'll come along, and when I give a lecture or a reading, you'll be there in the last row, just as you were today — and don't ever disappear again."

"The world according to you and me. Are we spending the rest of our lives in a cocoon? Can we be this foolish?"

"Do you mean what happens when we wake up from this? No idea. But I want to change so many things about myself."

"Such as?" she asked.

I had always wanted a leather jacket, just like hers. And I always wanted clothes that didn't make me look like a Sundayfied churchgoer who's removed his necktie on the way to the golf course. And I wanted to change my name to my nickname, and what did she think if I shaved my head or wore an earring. Above all I wanted to stop writing history — maybe a novel.

"Anything!"

"Let's never wake up from this."

We were walking up Via Giulia. She was right. It was deserted and I loved the absolute silence and the glazed sheen on the *sampietrini* at night and the one or two streetlights that cast their exiguous orange spill over Rome. My son had told me once about Rome by night. I'd never seen it this way before.

"So when did you know — about me?" she asked.

"I told you already."

"Then tell me again."

"On the train. I noticed you right away. But I didn't want to look. The whole grumpy thing was a sham. And you?"

"On the train too. *There's a man who knows life,* I thought, I didn't want us to stop talking."

"Little did you know."

"Little did I know I'd be walking down this street still wet with you."

"The things you say. I smell of you all over."

She reached over to my neck and licked it. "You do make me love who I am." Then on further thought: "I hope the day never comes when you make me hate myself. Now tell me again when you knew about us."

"There was also this other moment by the fish stand," I continued, "when you kept pointing at the fish you wanted and had craned your body forward, which was when I glimpsed your neck, your cheek, your ear, and caught myself wanting to caress every part of exposed skin from your breastbone up. I even thought of you naked making love to me. Then I pushed it away — *What's the use,* I thought."

"So what's the nickname you want to be called by?"

"It's not Sami," I said. Then I told her. No one had called me this since I was nine or ten except for old relatives and distant cousins, some of whom are still alive. When I write to them, I still sign my name that way. Otherwise they wouldn't know who I was.

After we were back, it would come to me in waves that night. This was still unreal — and there was nothing to compare it to — unreal because I knew enough to fear such fevers never last — unreal because it made everything around me feel equally frail, my life, my friends, my relatives, my work, myself.

We were lying very close together. "One body," she said. "Except when we eat or go to the bathroom," I added. "Not even!" she quipped. And with each of us coiled into the other with a thigh between the other's thighs, closing my eyes for a while, I began to see how this was altogether different from how it had been with so many women I'd known in my life and how our bodies themselves could be so ductile to everything we asked and sought of them, provided we asked and sought. What baffled me most, when I remembered the years of my life, was the distance we travel to lock our doors after scarcely leaving them ajar on our very first night with a stranger. She was right about this: the more we know someone, the more we shut the doors between us — not the other way around. "The thing that scares me," I began with my eyes still shut. "The thing that scares you?" she asked, already seeming to deride what I was about to tell her. "Of the two of us —" I started, but she stopped me right away. "Don't say it, don't," she cried, suddenly releasing herself from my embrace and shoving a palm almost violently over my mouth. At first I wasn't sure, but moments later, even as I relished the swiftness of her gesture, I tasted blood in my mouth. "I'm so, so sorry, I didn't mean to hurt or to offend you," she exclaimed. "It's not that." "Then what is it?" So I told her there was blood in my mouth and that it reminded me of sparring with a schoolmate in kindergarten and tasting something strange in my mouth and knowing for the first time that it must be blood. "I like the taste because of you." It took me all the way back to beginnings. And suddenly I saw it: I'd been alone for ever so long, even when I thought I wasn't alone — and the taste of something as real as blood was far, far better than the taste of just nothing, of wasted and barren years, so many years. "Then hit me," she said all of a sudden. "Are you mad?" "I want you to hit me back." "What, so we're even?" "No, because I want you to slap me on the face." "What for?" "Just slap me, for God's sake, and stop asking so many questions. Haven't you ever slapped anyone before?" "No," I said, almost apologizing for not having hurt a fly, let alone another human being. "Then do this!" And with these three words she struck her cheek savagely with the flat of her hand. "This is how it's done. Now do it!" I aped the gesture and gave her face a soft tap. "Harder, much, much harder, front and backhand." So I slapped her once, which startled her, but she straightaway turned the other cheek, to indicate that I should slap the other as well, which I did, and she said, "Again." "I don't like hurting people," I said. "Yes, but now we are as close as people who've lived three hundred years together, it's your language too, whether you like it or not. You love the taste, I love it too, now kiss me." She kissed me and I kissed her. "Did I hurt you?" "Never mind. Did it make you hard?" "Yes." "Good." "My lighthouse," she gasped, reaching down my body and holding me firmly. "This is who we'll be even when we're seen fully clothed and prettified in public, you inside me, all cum and juices."

"And don't fool yourself, this isn't honey-moon sex," she had said when we sat at the *enoteca* that she'd meant to show me. We had found a table in the corner and ordered two glasses of red. Then a plate of goat cheeses, and once done with the cheeses, a plate of cold cuts, and then two more glasses of wine. "This is how I want us always to be."

"Twelve hours ago we were complete strangers. I was a man drifting to sleep and you were the lady with the lapdog."

I looked around the place. I'd never been there before.

"Tell me something, anything," she said.

"I love seeing Rome through your eyes. I want to come back here tomorrow night with you."

"Me too," she said.

Neither of us said another word. We were among the very last to leave before closing time.

There were few hotel guests this time of year, and the personnel dressed in white jackets the next morning were busy confabulating and joking with one another while cheesy loud music was playing in the background.

"I hate background music and I hate their yapping," she said, indicating the help. She did not hesitate in turning around to one of the waiters who happened to be close by to ask if they could lower their voices. He was startled by the complaint but did not answer or apologize; he simply cowered and walked back to where another waiter and two waitresses were standing chuckling loudly. Right away they got quiet.

"I've grown to hate this hotel," I said, "but I come here each time I'm in Rome because of the balcony attached to my room. On warm days, I love sitting under the umbrella to read. Later in the evening I have drinks with friends either on my balcony or in the larger terrace upstairs above the third floor. It's simply heavenly there."

After breakfast, we crossed the bridge and were about to head toward the Aventine but then changed our minds and came back along the Lungotevere. It was still early Saturday morning, and Rome was very quiet. "There used to be a movie theater here." "It closed ages ago." "And there used to be a bric-a-brac shop hereabouts somewhere. I bought a small backgammon set once, made in Syria, all inlaid mother-of-pearl mosaics. A friend borrowed it, then broke it or lost it — I never saw it again." She sought my hand as we ambled near Campo de' Fiori. Nearby, the fish vendor was busy setting up. The wine store still hadn't opened. It felt like ages since we'd come here to buy fish.

"We're spending the week here in Rome," she told her father when he opened the door to us. She had bought enough food to last him three weeks.

"Nice!" he stuttered, scarcely disguising his joy. "And what will the two of you be doing for a whole week?"

"Don't know. Eating, taking pictures, visiting, being together."

"Strolling," I added. It was clear her father had understood we were lovers and wasn't shocked, or at least pretended not to be. You could read it on his face: *Yesterday you were strangers on a train and barely touching . . . and now you're fucking my daughter. Nice! She'll never change.*

"Where will you stay?" he asked Miranda.

"With him. It's five minutes away on foot from here, so you'll see me more than you've ever bargained for."

"And this is bad news?"

"It's great news. Can I leave the dog with you though?"

"But what about your work?"

"All I need is my cameras. Plus, I'm tired of the Far East. Maybe I can discover parts of Rome or northern Italy through *his* eyes. Yesterday we saw Villa Albani, which I'd never even seen before."

"I also want to take her to see the Archaeological Museum in Naples. The statue of Dirce being tied to a bull by two brothers needs an expert's camera."

"When are we going to Naples?"

"If you want, tomorrow," I said.

"More train rides. Perfect." She seemed truly overjoyed.

When Miranda left the room, her father

took me aside: "She's not all she's cracked up to be, you know. She's impulsive, and there's always a tempest brewing inside her head, but she is more delicate than the most friable china. Please be good to her, and be patient."

There was nothing to say to this. I stared at her father then smiled, and finally placed my hand on his. It was meant to reassure him, a gesture imparting warmth, silence, and friendship. I hoped it didn't seem patronizing.

Lunch was quiet and mostly an extension of breakfast. Miranda made a large omelet. How did he want his, she asked. "Plain," he said. "Maybe some spices?" she asked. He liked spices. "And not a dry omelet this time, please. Gennarina makes terrible omelets."

It had gotten warm and we had lunch on the terrace again. "And the walnuts?" he said afterward.

"The walnuts, of course."

She went back inside, took out the large bowl of walnuts then stepped into the library, where she found the book she was looking for and said she'd read for twenty minutes.

I had never read Chateaubriand, but on hearing her, determined that this was what

I wanted for the rest of my life. Every day, just after lunch, while sipping coffee as we were doing now, if she wanted and wasn't busy, twenty minutes of this great Frenchman's prose would make my day.

When we had drunk our coffee, her father did not accompany us to the door; instead he stayed on the terrace, seated at his table, and watched us leave.

"It mustn't be easy for him," I said as she shut the door behind her.

"Actually it's awful. And shutting this door behind me is always agony."

On our way to Piazza di San Cosimato, she looked at the darkening sky and said, "Looks like rain soon. Let's go back."

It was too early to head back to the hotel, so we strolled into a large housewares store. "Let's buy two identical mugs, one with your initials, and one with mine," she said.

She insisted on buying the mugs, mine with a large *M*, hers a large *S*. But she wasn't satisfied. "How about tattoos? I want you permanently inscribed on my body. Like a watermark. I want a tiny lighthouse. How about you?"

I thought for a moment.

"A fig."

"Tattoos then? I know of a place," she said.

I looked at her. *Why am I not even hesitating?*

"Where on our bodies?" I asked.

"Next to . . . you know."

"Left or right?"

"Right."

"Right it is."

She was silent a moment.

"Is this going too fast for you?"

"I love that it is. Will it hurt?"

"I wouldn't know. I've never gotten a tattoo before. Never even had my ears pierced. What I know is that I want our bodies never to be the same again."

"We'll sit and watch each other get tattoos," I said. "Then when I go to meet my Maker and am asked to get naked and expose myself and he sees this fig tattoo to the right of my junk, what do you think he'll say? 'Professor, what's this next to your flibbertigibbet?' 'A tattoo,' I'll say. 'A fig tattoo, is it?' 'Yes, Lord.' 'And the reason for disfiguring the body that took nine long months to make?' 'Passion is the reason.' 'Yes, and?' he says. 'I wanted a sign carved on my body to show I wanted everything changed, starting with my body. Because for once in my life I knew there'd be no regrets. Maybe it was also my way of marking my body with something that I always

137

feared might otherwise vanish as easily as it breezed in. So I carved her symbol on me to remember. If You could tattoo my soul with her name, You should do it right now. You see, God — may I call You this? — I was on the point of giving up, of living the life of someone who had accepted his sentence, and cowering before his menial little lot, living as if life were an extended waiting room far below room temperature, when suddenly here was this beautiful commutation — I know I'm using big words, but I trust You understand, Lord — and from the dark, silent, muddy, narrow, shanty lane that was my life it swelled into a huge mansion facing a wide-open field with beach views all around and large rooms with large, flung-open windows that never rattle and never shake or slam shut when a sea breeze wafts through a house that has never seen darkness since the day You lit the first match and knew that light was good.' "

"So you're a comedian! What does God do then?"

"God lets me in, of course. 'You're in, good man,' he says. But then I ask, 'Pardon, Your Lordship, but what good is heaven to me now?'

" 'Heaven is heaven. It doesn't get better than this. Have you any idea what people have given up to live here? Want to take a look at the alternative? I can show you. In fact, I can take you down there and show you where you could just as easily be skewered and roasted for having that piece of nonsense punctured you know where. But you're pouting. Why?' 'Why, Lord? Because I'm here and she's over there.' 'What? Do you want her to die too so that you can coddle and canoodle and have your little fun-and-slop in my kingdom?' 'I don't want her to die.' 'Are you jealous that she's likely to find someone else, because find someone else she will.' 'I don't mind that either.' 'Then what, my good man?' 'It's that I would love one more hour, one measly hour in the million trillion bazillion hours of eternity to be with her, a tiny speck of nothing in the realm of unending time. It costs You nothing, I just want to go back to that Friday night at our *enoteca,* holding hands over the table as they keep serving us wine and cheese as the place empties out while only lovers and very close friends stay behind and all I want is a chance to tell her that what happened between us, if it lasted twenty-four hours, was worth the wait of untold light-years that came before evolution even started, and are to follow after our dust is no longer even dust, until that day in a quadrillion years on some other planet in some distant constellation a Sami and Miranda will happen again. I wish them my very best. But for now, good Lord, all I ask for is another hour.' 'But don't you see?' he'll say. 'What don't I see?' 'Don't you see that you already had your hour. And I didn't just give you an hour, I gave you twenty-four of them. Do you have any idea how difficult it was for me to let your organs do what they may normally fail to do once at your age, let alone twice?' 'Correction: three times it was, good Lord, three times.' He pauses for a few seconds. 'And besides, if I give you an hour now, you'll want a day, and if I give you a day, you'll want a year. I know your type.'

"Right now, God seems to have offered me more time. It's not official, and He'll deny it if I tell anyone but you. You'll love my home on the beach. Every day we'll take long walks in the countryside, swim, and eat fruit, lots of fruit. We'll watch old movies and listen to music. I'll even play the piano for you in the small parlor and let you hear again and again that wonderful moment in Beethoven's sonata when suddenly the tempest subsides in the first movement and all you hear is the trickle patter of slow, very slow notes, and then silence before something like a storm erupts again. We'll be like Myrrha and Cinyras, except Cinyras won't try to kill his daughter for having slept with him, and she won't run away from her father's bed and turn into a tree, and if we're truly lucky, in nine months, like Myrrha, you'll give birth to Adonis."

"I am my beloved's, and my beloved is mine. And how long does this idyll last?"

"Do we need to know? No limits."

The tattoo artist was booked for the day. So we dropped the idea. Instead we ambled about until we decided to head back to the hotel. In our room: "I cannot believe how beautiful you are. Tell me what you like about me . . . Is there anything?" I asked. "I don't know. If I could open your body and slip into it and sew you back from the inside, I would do it, so I could cradle your quiet dreams and let you dream mine. I'd be the rib that hasn't become me yet, happy to hang on and, as you said, see the world with your eyes, not mine, and hear you echo my thoughts and think they're yours." She sat down on the bed and began unbuckling my belt. "I haven't done this in a while." Then she unzipped my fly and took off her clothes and stared deep in my eyes with a gaze that said if love had never existed on

141

this planet, it was born in this tiny, rinky-dink so-called boutique hotel bedroom facing a narrow street and so many windows where people are welcome to look in. "Kiss me now," she said, reminding me how lucky I was to see this raw, savage, unkempt, gritty moment suddenly in my life. After our long kiss, she looked at me with something verging on defiance. "Now you know," she said. "Do you believe me?" she finally asked. "I've given you everything I have, and what I haven't given means nothing, just nothing. The question is what more will I have to give next week, and will you even want it?"

"Then give me less. I'll accept a half, or a quarter, or an eighth. Shall I go on?" A while later: "I can't go back to my life. And I don't want you to go back to yours, Sami. The only good memory I have of my father's home is of you in it. I want to go back to that moment when you held my hands as I was fixing your collar and I kept thinking, *This man likes me, he does like me, why doesn't he kiss me, then?* Instead I watched you struggle until you finally touched my forehead, like a child, and then I thought, *He thinks I'm too young.*"

"No, I'm too old — that's what I thought."

"You're such a fool." She stood up and removed the paper wrapping around each mug. "They're lovely."

"I have the house, you have the mugs, the rest is just details. Every day at lunch we'll eat the same frugal foods: tomatoes, cut into quarters, with country bread I love to bake, basil, fresh olive oil, a can of sardines, unless you broil a fish for us, eggplants from the garden, and for dessert fresh figs in late summer and persimmons in the fall, berries in wintertime, and whatever else grows on trees — peaches, plums, and apricots. I am so eager to play for you that short pianissimo from Beethoven's sonata. Let us spend our time this way, until you grow bored and tired of me. And if before that you'll expect a child, we'll stay together until my time is up, and then we'll both know. And there will be no sorrow from me, and none from you, because you'll know as I'll know that whatever time you've given me, my entire life, from childhood, school years, university, my years as a professor, a writer, and all the rest that happened was all leading up to you. And that's good enough for me."

"Why?"

"Because you've made me love this, just this. I was never a big fan of planet Earth, and didn't set great store in this other thing called life, but the thought of eating tomatoes with salt and oil at lunch and drinking chilled white wine as we're sitting stark naked on our balcony basking in the early noonday sun watching the sea, sends shivers down my spine this very moment."

Then a thought crossed my mind. "If I were thirty years old would any of this have been more tempting?"

"None of it would have happened if you were thirty years old."

"You're not answering my question."

"If you were my age, I'd pretend I was happy, I'd pretend I loved my career, your career, our life, but I'd be faking it as I've been faking it with everyone I've known. My problem is discovering what not faking is — and this is difficult and scary for me, because my bearings are always pitched to who I ought to be, not to who I am, to what I should have, not to what I never knew I craved, to life as I found it, not to the life I've let myself think was only a dream. You're oxygen to me, and I've been living off methane."

We lay on top of the bedspread, which she said had probably never been washed. "Any idea how many people have lain on this as naked and sweaty as we are now?"

We laughed it off. Without saying anything we showered for the first time since we'd met on the train and got dressed to meet Elio.

Elio was standing by the entrance of the hotel. We hugged, then after I released him he noticed that the person standing next to me was not a stranger who happened to be stepping out of the hotel at the same time as I was. Miranda right away extended her arm and they shook hands. "I'm Miranda," she said. "Elio," he replied. They both smiled at each other. "I've heard so much about you," she said. "All he does is talk about you." He laughed. "He exaggerates, there's so little to tell." As we walked out of the pebbled courtyard, Elio gave me a discreetly quizzical look that meant *Who is she?* She intercepted the questioning glance, and said right away: "I'm the person he slept with after picking me up on the train yesterday." He laughed, though slightly uncomfortably. Then she added: "Had you been waiting for him at Termini yesterday I wouldn't be standing here telling you this." She immediately took her camera and asked us to stand by the gate. "I want to do this," she said.

"She's a photographer," I explained, almost by way of apology.

"So what should we do?" asked my son,

who was a bit at a loss for how to proceed.

Miranda sized up the situation right away. "I know the two of you have your vigils to perform, so I don't want to intrude," she said, emphasizing the word *vigil* to show that she was already familiar with our father-son lingo. "But I can tag along and I swear, I won't utter a word."

"Promise not to laugh at us, though," he said, "because we *are* ridiculous."

It was the way we walked — together yet not together — that allowed a touch of awkwardness to stand between us. I was trying to keep in step with her without letting him think that his place in my life was in any way altered or diminished by her presence; but then, a few steps farther, I caught myself walking much closer to him, almost on the verge of neglecting her. I was also worried that he might resent her presence and had wanted to talk about important personal matters. And perhaps he wasn't ready to meet her yet, and certainly not so suddenly. He must have noticed my discomfort and tactfully began walking ahead of us. I knew he was doing it on purpose, almost deferring to her, because we normally walked elbow to elbow. If there was tension between the three of us, his move helped defuse it and restored the comradeship we felt while crossing the bridge together.

We had spoken of going on foot to the Protestant Cemetery, but it was cloudy and it was already getting late. The cemetery is perfect on a sunny, quiet weekday morning, I said, not a bustling Saturday afternoon. So we decided to repeat our walk on Via Giulia and headed to a café we all knew.

On our way I asked Elio what he'd played the night before, and he told us Mozart's E-flat Major and D Minor concerti with an orchestra from Ljubljana. He'd had to practice throughout the night before the concert, and all during the day itself. But it had gone very well. He had to be in Naples for another concert Sunday afternoon.

"So which vigil shall we start with today?" asked Miranda. "Or will it be a surprise?"

Once again I worried that vigils were to be celebrated between us only, not with a third person. So to lighten the mood, I told him that I'd cheated and had already done one vigil with Miranda: the third-floor apartment on Roma Libera where I'd lived as a young teacher.

"The chick with the oranges?" he asked.

It made all three of us laugh.

"Wasn't there another vigil on Via Margutta?" asked Miranda.

"Yes, but let's not do her today."

"Actually, the café where we're headed is sort of vigilly," said Elio.

"Whose vigil, yours or Sami's?" she asked.

"Well, we're not sure," I said. "It started by being Elio's, then by dint of coming back here with him, it became mine too, and in the end ours. So you could say that we've overwritten and lived each other's memories. Which is why coming here means something more, something extra for which even the professor in me has no words. And now, Miranda, you're in these vigils too."

"See, this is what I love about him," she said, turning to Elio, "the way his mind twists everything, as if life were made up of meaningless scraps of paper that turn into tiny origami models the moment he starts folding them. Are you this way as well?"

"I'm his son." He nodded self-consciously.

Caffè Sant'Eustachio was so crowded that we were unable to find a table and decided to drink our coffees at the bar. Elio added that in all the years he'd been coming here, he'd never once had a chance to sit down. Tourists spend hours occupying all the seats, reading maps and guidebooks. He insisted on treating. While he slid between the throng of customers who were either waiting to order or to pay at the cashier, she

148

sidled up to me and asked, "Do you think I shocked him?"

"Not at all."

"Do you think he minds I'm barging in?"

"I can't see how. He's been pestering me to find someone after my divorce."

"And have you found someone?"

"I think I have. She said she'd stay with me."

"Who's going to stay with you?" asked Elio, carrying a receipt and struggling to catch the attention of one of the men behind the espresso machines.

"She is."

"Have you told her what she's getting into?"

"No. She'll be horrified soon enough."

Seconds later three cups were placed on the counter in front of us.

"I came here three years ago trying to have a private vigil with a girl and it was a disaster," said Elio.

"How so?" asked Miranda.

Elio explained that as he was trying to experience her presence at the café as something meaningful, especially since the place already bore the imprint of other events in his life, they had an argument. She kept saying that there was nothing special about the kind of coffee they brewed here, he countered by saying that this was not about the coffee at all but about being here to have the coffee. Their disagreement not only ruined the vigil but made him hate her. They sipped their coffee as fast as they could and walked out in separate directions and never saw each other again.

"Yet quite a few years ago here is where I had my first inkling of what my life as an artist living among artists would be like. My father and I come here each time he's in Rome."

"And have your years as an artist been what you expected?" Miranda asked.

"I'm superstitious, so I should watch what I say," he replied, "but they've been very reassuring — my years as a pianist, that is. The rest, well, we don't discuss the rest."

"And yet it's the rest I want to know about," I said, catching myself almost echoing Miranda's father. At this point, Miranda recognized that the conversation was veering to the personal and excused herself to look for the bathroom.

"The rest, Dad," he went on, "is a closed book these days. But the first time I came here I was seventeen and I was with people who read a lot, loved poetry, were deeply involved in cinema, and knew all there is to know about classical music. They inducted me into their clan and every vacation I had from school and later from university I'd come to Rome to stay with them and just learn."

I said nothing, but he caught the look in my eye.

"But more than my friendship with them, you above everyone else made me who I am today. We never had secrets you and I, you know about me, and I know about you. In this I consider myself the luckiest son on earth. You taught me how to love — how to love books, music, beautiful ideas, people, pleasure, even myself. Better yet you taught me that we have one life only and that time is always stacked against us. This much I know, young as I am. It's just that I forget the lesson sometimes."

"Why are you telling me this?" I asked.

"Because I can see you now — not as my father, but as a man in love. I've never seen you like this. It makes me very happy, almost envious to see you. You are so young suddenly. It must be love."

If it hadn't occurred to me until then, I knew now that I was indeed the luckiest father alive. People were milling around us, some trying to wedge their way to the counter. None of them seemed to intrude on our intimate moment together. We were having a quiet fireside chat in one of Rome's most bustling cafés.

"Love is easy," I said. "It's the courage to love and to trust that matters, and not all of us have both. But what you may not know is that you taught me far more than I've taught you! These vigils, for instance, are perhaps nothing more than my desire to tread in your footsteps, to share with you anything and everything and be in your life as I always want you to be in mine. I've taught you how to earmark moments where time stops, but these moments mean very little unless they're echoed in someone you love. Otherwise they stay in you and either fester all through your life or, if you're lucky — and very few are — you're able to pass them on in something called art, in your case music. But above all it was always your courage I envied, how you trusted your love for music and later your love for Oliver."

At that moment, Miranda was back among us and put her arm around me.

"I never had that trust, either in my loves or, if you'd believe it, in my work," I continued, "but I found it almost inadvertently the moment this young lady invited me to lunch yesterday, while all I kept saying to her was, *No thank you, no, I couldn't possibly, no, no* — but she didn't believe me, and she didn't let me coil back into my little conch."

I was glad we'd spoken. "As you said, we have never had secrets, you and I. I hope we never do."

We left Sant'Eustachio after quickly gulping our three sips of coffee each and were headed toward the Corso.

"So where to next?" asked Miranda.

"I suppose Via Belsiana," I guessed, remembering that Elio and I always ended up on Via Belsiana to do what he called the *If Love* walk to a bookstore, in memory of a book of poems published ten years earlier.

"No, not Via Belsiana today. I want to take you somewhere I've never taken you before."

"Is this recent then?" I asked, hoping he'd let me in on his latest romance.

"Not recent at all. But it marks a moment where for a short while I held life in my hands and was never the same afterward. Sometimes I think that my life stopped here and will only restart here."

He seemed absorbed in thought. "I have no idea if Miranda is up for this and perhaps neither are you. But we've confided enough already not to stop now. So let me take you there. It's just a two-minute walk away."

When we reached Via della Pace I thought he was about to take us to one of my favorite churches in the area. Instead, no sooner had we sighted the church than he made a right turn and took us to Via Santa Maria dell'Anima. Then, after a few steps, and just as I'd done with Miranda the day before, he stopped at a corner where a very old lamp was built into a wall. "I never told you this, Dad, but I was drunk out of my mind one night, I had just vomited by the statue of the Pasquino and couldn't have been more dazed in my life yet here as I leaned against this very wall, I knew, drunk as I was, that this, with Oliver holding me, was my life, that everything that had come beforehand with others was not even a rough sketch or the shadow of a draft of what was happening to me. And now ten years later, when I look at this wall under this old streetlamp, I am back with him and I swear to you, nothing has changed. In thirty, forty, fifty years I will feel no differently. I have met many women and more men in my life, but what is watermarked on this very wall overshadows everyone I've known. When I come to be here, I can be alone or with people, with you for instance, but I am always with him. If I stood for an hour staring at this wall, I'd be with him for an hour. If I spoke to this wall, it would speak back."

"What would it say?" asked Miranda, totally taken in by the thought of Elio and the wall.

"What would it say? Simple: 'Look for me, find me.' "

"And what do you say?"

"I say the same thing. 'Look for me, find me.' And we're both happy. Now you know."

"Maybe what you need is less pride and more courage. Pride is the nickname we give fear. You were afraid of nothing once. What happened?"

"You're wrong about my courage," he said. "I've never even had the courage to call him, to write to him, much less to visit him. All I can do when I'm alone is whisper his name in the dark. But then I laugh at myself. I just pray I'll never whisper it when I'm with someone else."

Miranda and I were quiet. She went up to him and kissed him on the cheek. There was nothing to say.

"Whispering someone's name happened to me only once, but I think it marked me for life," I said, turning to Miranda, who right away understood.

"In his case . . . but can I tell him?" she asked me.

I nodded.

"In his case he whispered another woman's name to the woman he was sleeping with," said Miranda. "What weird families we all belong to!"

There was nothing to add.

Minutes later we decided to head off for a glass of wine at Sergetto's.

We arrived just as the *enoteca* was opening and had our choice of tables, so we sat where we'd sat the night before. "See, I caught the vigil bug as well," said Miranda. I liked that not all the lights were lit and that the place was dim, which made it seem later than it was. The man at the bar recognized us right away and asked if we wanted the same red. I asked Elio if a Barbaresco was good for him as well. He nodded, then reminded us that this evening he was driving back to Naples with a friend. He had come all the way to Rome to see me.

"What kind of a friend?" I asked.

"A friend with a car," he answered, miming a dry look and shaking his head, meaning I was totally on the wrong track.

When the wine arrived, the waiter went back to the counter and brought some snacks. "On the house," he said.

"Must be because I tipped him nicely last night. We were probably the very last to leave before they closed."

We toasted one another's happiness.

"You never know, we might come to tomorrow's concert after we go to the Archaeological Museum — if we do go."

"Please, please do. I'll have two tickets for you waiting at the box office." Then he put on his sweater and stood up. "I will say one thing. You said it to me once years ago, now it's my turn: I envy the two of you. Please don't ruin it."

I was with the two people I cared for the most in the world.

We kissed goodbye. Then I sat down again facing Miranda. "I think I am extremely happy."

"Same here. We could do this for the rest of our lives."

"We could."

"What's the first thing you want to do next week when we'll be at the beach if the weather holds?"

"I want to take a taxi at the train station, get home, put on a bathing suit, climb down the rocks, and dive with you into the water."

"I left my bathing suit in Florence."

"There are plenty in the house. Better yet: we'll swim in the nude."

"In November?"

"In November the water's still warm."

CADENZA

"You're blushing," he said.

"No, I'm not."

He gave an amused, disbelieving glance from across the table. "Are you sure?"

I thought for a few seconds and then gave in. "I guess I am, aren't I?"

I was young enough to hate being read so easily, especially during an awkward silence with someone who was close to twice my age, but I was sufficiently grown-up to welcome having a blush say something I was reluctant to disclose. Then I looked at him.

"You're blushing too," I said.

"I know."

This was about two hours later.

I'd met him during intermission at a chamber music concert at the Church of Sainte U. on the Right Bank. It was an early-November Sunday, not chilly, but not warm, just your basic overcast autumnal evening that starts too early and presages

161

the long winter months to come. Many in the audience were already seated inside the church and were wearing gloves; others hadn't removed their coats. Yet despite the chill there was something snug in the air, as people quietly made their way down the pews, clearly in anticipation of the music. It was my first time inside this church and I had chosen a seat in the very back, in case the playing wasn't to my liking and I wanted to leave without disturbing anyone.

I was curious to hear what might be the very last performance of the Florian Quartet. The youngest member must have been in his late seventies. They played regularly in that church, but I had never heard them live before and knew them only from their rare, out-of-print recorded music and a few performances on the Web. They had just finished playing a Haydn quartet and after intermission were going to play Beethoven's C-sharp Minor. Unlike the others in church — and there were no more than forty or so in attendance that Sunday — I was a latecomer and had bought my ticket from one of the nuns seated at a small table by the entrance. Almost everyone else had gotten theirs by mail and entered the church holding large vouchers, which they'd been asked to keep unfolded while a hunched, elderly nun dutifully copied everyone's full name with an old green fountain pen. She was at least eighty years old and must have been doing this for ages, probably with the same pen and in the same tremulous, archaic script. The small bar code numbers on the vouchers probably reflected the younger image that the church wanted to project to new parishioners, but the old nun was having a hard time recopying them before stamping each voucher. No one said anything about her slow pace but there were a few indulgent smiles exchanged among those who hadn't had their vouchers validated.

During the intermission, I was waiting in line by the entrance for mulled cider, which the same nun was now scrupulously dispensing into plastic cups with a ladle she was barely able to lift when it was full. Everyone donated much more than the €1 written on a paper sign on the bulletin board next to the large vat of hot cider. I was never a fan of mulled cider, but everyone else seemed to be, so I stood there and when my turn came, I put five euros into her bowl, for which she thanked me profusely. The old nun was sharp. She could tell it was my first time in her church and asked if I'd enjoyed the Haydn. I uttered an enthusiastic yes.

He had been standing in front of me in line, and after I paid for my cider, he simply turned around and asked, "Why is someone so young interested in the Florian Quartet? They are so old." Then, perhaps realizing that the question had dropped from nowhere, he added, "The second violin — must be in his eighties. The others are hardly any younger."

He was tall, slim, elegantly put together, with a gray mane of hair that fringed the collar of his blue blazer.

"I've been interested in the cellist and I figured that as it's rumored they're traveling later this year before possibly disbanding, our paths might never cross again. So here I am."

"Doesn't someone your age have better things to do?"

"Someone my age?" I asked, surprise and stung irony in my tone.

A moment of silence hung awkwardly between us. He shrugged his shoulders, probably his way of apologizing without saying anything, and seemed about to turn and walk to the area by the two portals where people were smoking, others chatting and stretching their legs. "Feet always get cold inside a church," he said as he turned around and headed to the door. It was a closing, throwaway sentence.

Then realizing I might have snubbed him with my tone, I asked, "Are you a fan of the Florian?"

"Not really. I'm not even a fan of chamber music. But I know quite a bit about them because my father loved classical music and subsidized their concerts in this church, and I've been doing the same now, though frankly I prefer jazz. But I come here because I used to tag along with him on Sunday evenings when I was young, and I still come every few weeks or so to sit and listen, and perhaps to imagine I'm with my father for a while — but I'm sure all this must seem a rather silly reason to sit and listen to their playing."

What instrument had his father played, I asked.

The piano.

"My father never played at home. But on weekends, when we'd stay in the country, he'd go to the other end of the house late at night and from my bedroom upstairs, I'd hear the piano as though it were being played by a furtive waif who'd stop the moment he heard footsteps creaking on the floorboards. He never spoke about his playing, nor did my mother ever bring it up, and the best I learned to do in the morning was to say I'd dreamed the piano was playing itself again. I think he wished he'd continued as a professional pianist, just as I'm sure he wished I'd grow to love classical music. He was the type who seldom forced his views on others, much less spoke to total strangers — totally unlike his son, as I'm sure you've noticed." At which he chuckled. "He was too tactful to ask me to join him on Sundays for these concerts, and was probably resigned to going alone. But my mother didn't want him out by himself at night, so she'd ask me to come with him. Eventually it became a habit. After the concert he'd buy me a pastry. We'd sit together at a place nearby, and, when I was a bit older, we'd head out afterward and have dinner. But he never spoke about his time as a pianist, and besides, my mind was altogether elsewhere in those years. Sunday evenings were always reserved for last-minute homework, so coming here with him meant I'd have to stay up doing work I could have finished much earlier. But I was glad to be with him, more than I liked the music, and as you see, I'm still bound by routine. I've spoken too much, haven't I."

"Do you play?" I asked, to let him know that I didn't mind his talking.

"Not really. I followed in my father's footsteps. He was a lawyer, his father was a lawyer, I became a lawyer. Neither my father nor I wanted to be lawyers, and yet . . . *Life!*" He smiled wistfully. It was the second time that he'd smiled and then shrugged his shoulders. His was a broad, endearing, and sudden smile that caught you off guard, but given the irony underscoring the word *life,* there was little mirth in it. "And which instrument do *you* play?" he asked, suddenly turning to me. I didn't want our conversation to end and was surprised to sense he didn't want it to either.

"Piano," I answered.

"Vocation or avocation?"

"Vocation. I hope."

He seemed to think for a while.

"Don't give up, young man, don't."

So saying he put a wise, gently patronizing arm around my shoulder. I don't know why, but I reached for the hand that had rested on my shoulder and touched it. It had happened so seamlessly that I looked at him and we both smiled, which allowed his hand, which would most likely have left the spot, to stay just a moment longer. He turned but then looked at me once more, and I felt a sudden urge to hurl myself against him and put my arms around his upper waist right under his jacket. He must have felt something along those lines as well, because in the awkward silence that followed what he'd just said, he kept staring and I was staring back, totally undaunted, until it hit me that perhaps I had read all the signals wrong and I began to want to look away. I liked that his eyes lingered on me still, it made me feel handsome and desirable, something soft, caressing that I wanted to hold in place and didn't want to escape from except by burrowing into his chest. I liked the promise, in his gaze, of something totally kind and guileless.

But then, perhaps to give a hasty justification to our smiles, he said, "You come here for the music and I come for my father. He died almost thirty years ago, yet nothing changes here." He chuckled. "Same cider, same odors, same old nuns, same stifling November evenings. Do you like November?"

"Sometimes, but not always."

"Me neither. I don't even like church, though perhaps I like to come here on evenings like this . . . and, well, *me voici,* here I am." I could sense he was running out of things to say and was fumbling to keep our conversation going. Then silence. Again the warm, fetching smile, a blend of wisdom, irony, and just a dab of sadness to remind me that there was nothing light about this gentle, possibly unhappy man.

When we saw the quartet shuffle back to their places and that it was time for the Beethoven, he asked where I was sitting. I didn't understand why he was asking, but I pointed to the corner seat in one of the last pews where I'd left my backpack and jacket.

"Chosen wisely." He understood why. "But don't slip away," he added. I thought he was asking me to give the quartet another chance before opting for a hasty exit but I had already changed my mind after the Haydn and had no intention of leaving before the end of the concert. But then to clear the air I asked point-blank: "Do you want me to wait for you?" The inflection in my voice could have been all wrong. I sounded as though I were asking an older person if he'd need someone to hold the door for him while he struggled with his walker. So I repeated: "I'll wait for you outside."

He didn't say anything; he simply nodded. But his wasn't a nod of affirmation, meaning yes; it was the pensive, distracted, wistful nod of someone who normally chooses not to believe a word he's heard.

"Yes, why not, wait for me," he finally

said. "And my name is Michel." I told him my name. We shook hands.

I was sure he was going to leave at the end of the first movement, but half an hour later we met on the steps of the church, just as we'd promised, except that I had a feeling he'd forgotten about our meeting. He was speaking with a couple, and all three seemed about to head out somewhere. But as soon as he saw me, he turned around, then hastily finished talking to them as they shook hands goodbye. He apologized for not introducing me. I was busy wrapping my scarf around my neck, which was my way of deflecting his apology. I caught myself trying to seem surprised he had waited or that he remembered we'd promised to meet. Or had he perhaps waited simply to say goodbye once more before we went our separate ways?

Instead, he suggested we go for a little something at a small bistro not too far across the bridge. I told him I had locked my folding bike nearby. Did he mind if I unlocked it and walked with it? Not at all. It was around ten on a Sunday evening, and the streets were largely empty. "And you are my guest," he added, to reassure me that money should not be a concern. I accepted. I liked the walk, especially as it had rained during the concert and the cobblestones glinted under the streetlights. "Just like a Brassaï photo," I said. "Yes, isn't it," he added. "And what do you do besides play the piano?"

I noticed that he tended to start some sentences with the word *and,* perhaps to smooth out the jolting or missing transition between unrelated subjects, especially when broaching something slightly more probing, more personal. I told him I taught at the conservatory. Did I like teaching? Very much. Then I said that once a week I also played gratis and for the fun of it at a piano bar in a luxury hotel. He didn't ask the name of the hotel. Tactful, I thought, or just his way of showing he wasn't the sort who prods or cares.

When we arrived at the bridge, we spotted two Brazilian performers, a man and a woman, singing to a large group who'd gathered around them. The man's voice was high, the woman's raucous. Together they sang beautifully. I stopped walking the bike and stood a moment, one hand holding the handlebar. He stood there as well, holding the other end of the handlebar, as if he were helping me steady the bike. I could tell he felt slightly awkward. When the young singers ended their song, everyone on the bridge clapped and cheered, while the two singers immediately launched into another duet. I wanted to hear part of the second song and wasn't budging, but soon after they had begun singing we decided to walk away and, once on the opposite bank, heard the crowd clapping when the singers were done. He saw me turn around, then turned himself to watch the male singer put down his guitar, while she began sauntering through the crowd, cap in hand. Did I recognize the song, he asked. Yes, I said. Did he? "Maybe, I think so." But I could tell he had no idea, just as he seemed out of his element listening to Brazilian music played on a bridge, of all places.

"It's about a man who comes back home from work and asks his beloved to get dressed and come outside and dance with him. There is such an eruption of joy on their street that eventually the whole city bursts with joy."

"Nice song," he said. I wanted him to feel less ill at ease and for a few seconds clasped his shoulder.

But he was totally at home once he opened the door to his bistro. The place was indeed small, just as he had said, but it also looked very exclusive. I should have known. His navy Forestière jacket, the large, flowing printed scarf, and the Corthay shoes were dead giveaways. Our little snack turned out to be a three-course dinner. He ordered a single malt, Caol Ila was his favorite, he said. He asked if I wanted one. I said yes but had no idea what a single malt was. I could tell he'd seen through this, perhaps had seen it many times. I liked his manner, but it left me feeling uneasy. He explained the menu. "Not too many meats here," he said. "But their wine cellar is good, and I like how they cook vegetables. Fish is also very good." He shut the menu no sooner than he'd opened it. "I always order the same thing, so I don't even bother to look." He waited for me to decide what I wanted. I couldn't decide. Then I did something that came to me totally impulsively. "Order for me," I said. I loved the idea, and it seemed he loved it too. "Easily done. I'll order what I always have for you too."

He called the waiter and ordered. Then after sipping from his whiskey, he said that his father, who had introduced him to this restaurant, was also in the habit of ordering the same thing all the time. "He was diabetic," he explained, "so I learned to avoid what diabetics shouldn't eat. No sugars, no rice, no pasta, no bread, and seldom any butter." As he said that, he was buttering and then sprinkling salt on the end of his small *pain Poilâne* roll, snickering as he brought it to his mouth. "I don't always walk in my father's footsteps, but his shadow is difficult to avoid. I am full of contradictions."

There was a pause. He went on about his father's regimen, but I wanted to hear more about his contradictions, which interested me and which might have told me more about who this man was and how he saw himself. He seemed to waver between opening up or going on about food and dieting. There was even a moment of slight tension, as though we both sensed we were just making conversation and could easily get trapped in small talk. To get past the awkwardness, I told him about my two great-uncles, whom I'd never met but who had the reputation of being very savvy bakers and who had opened three bakeries in Milan only to be rounded up as socialists during the war. "They ended up in Birkenau. My mother frequently spoke about her uncles when I was growing up. They too, as in your father's case, cast long shadows on my mother's family."

"What kind of shadows?" he asked, not quite getting my point.

"She bakes wonderful cakes."

He gave a hearty laugh. I was glad he got the joke. "But I know: some shadows never go away," I added.

"You're right. My father's shadow never left me. He died two years after I inherited his law practice. I was your age at the time." But then he stopped short again and thought a while, as though he had seized an unforeseen link between what he'd just said and what, without my knowing, must have been pressing on his mind. "And you know that I'm almost twice your age."

This was when I blushed. It was a tense and awkward moment, partly because he had broached a subject that felt totally premature and too close to what we were cautiously sidestepping, crossing t's that weren't even written out yet and should have remained silent, at least for a while longer. But his statement also left me feeling at a loss for what to say, and, as I rummaged for just the right words, the blush must have signaled my discomfort. Perhaps it was his way of bringing the subject out into the open and making me say something to allay his own anxieties. I struggled to banish our silence but couldn't. Finally, "You don't show your age at all," I said, my attempt at an evasive response.

"That is not what I meant" was his quick

comeback.

"I know what you meant." And to show there was no misunderstanding between us: "I wouldn't be sitting here with you, would I?" Was I blushing again? I hoped not. The silence that suddenly hovered between us did not displease him, and he nodded again, that same wistful and reflective nod, followed by a very mild shaking of the head, not of negation but of something bordering on disbelief and speechless wonderment at the way life simply plays along sometimes. "I didn't mean to make things awkward for you."

He was apologizing.

Or maybe not.

It was my turn to shake my head.

"No awkwardness at all," I said. Then, after a short pause, "And now you're the one blushing."

He pursed his lips. I reached for his hand across the table and held it for a moment in a friendly gesture, hoping he wouldn't feel uneasy. He didn't withdraw it.

"You don't believe in fate, do you?" he asked.

"I don't know," I said. "I've never really thought about it."

It was the kind of talk that was not as oblique as I would have wished. I could sense where he was headed, and I didn't mind the candor; but I didn't need the matter discussed too broadly either. Perhaps he belonged to a generation that sought out what was a tad difficult to discuss, I to one where what's obvious enough is left unstated. I was used to the totally direct approach that requires no words whatsoever, or just a glance or a hasty text. But shrouded, lingering speech left me unmoored.

"So if it wasn't fate, what brought you to the concert tonight?"

He gave my question some thought, then, looking down and away from me, started drawing ridges on the tablecloth with the fork he hadn't yet used. They looked like light furrows that made sudden squiggly turns around his bread plate. He was so taken by what had crossed his mind that I was sure he was no longer focusing on my question, which I welcomed, since on second thought I hoped he'd let go of our gingerly back-and-forth. But then he looked up at me and said that the answer to my question couldn't be simpler.

"What is it?" I asked, knowing he'd say something about his father.

Instead he said, "You."

"Me?"

He nodded. "Yes, you."

"But you didn't know you'd meet me."

"A meaningless detail. Fate works forward, backward, and crisscrosses sideways and couldn't care less how we scan its purposes with our rickety little befores and afters."

I took this in. "Too, too deep for me." There was another moment of silence between us.

"You see, my father believed in fate," he went on.

What a generous soul, I thought. He had sensed I wanted to skirt the subject and had deftly brought the conversation back to his father. But I wasn't really listening — he could tell I wasn't. Then he stopped. He was probably still debating how to broach the unspoken between us, which explains why he cast a lingering glance at me, then looked away. What totally surprised me, though, was what he said next as we stood up from our table and were about to leave. "Will I see you again? I would like to."

His question startled me. I muttered a feeble but all too hasty "Yes, of course." My reply came so quickly that it must have sounded totally disingenuous. I had expected something far bolder than a goodbye from him.

"But only if you want to," he added.

I stared at him. "You know I'd like to."
And this wasn't the single malt or the wine
speaking.

He nodded his signature nod. He was not
convinced. But not displeased.

"Same church, same time next Sunday,
then."

I did not venture to add anything more.
So tonight was not in the cards, I thought.

We were the very last to leave the restaurant. It was clear from the way the waiters
were hovering that they were eager to close
down the moment we stepped outside.

On the sidewalk, we instinctively embraced. But it was a makeshift, clumsy hug
that was more like a holding back than the
prolonged cuddle I had hoped to find in his
arms earlier on when we'd met during
intermission. He was already softening his
hold. Once again I felt an impulse to throw
myself against him and put my arms around
him and, though I held back, in the flurry
of the moment, I ended up kissing him not
on the cheek, but without meaning to,
under both his ears. Definitely the single
malt and the wine this time. I am sure he
must have noticed. But I liked what I'd
done. Then I thought twice about it. This
was awkward, I thought. More awkward yet
when I spotted the three waiters staring out

the window from behind the parted muslin sheers. They knew him well and must have witnessed similar scenes many times before.

He walked me to where I'd locked my bicycle, watched me unlock it, started a bit of small talk about the diminutive size of the bike, even said he'd thought of purchasing one just like it. But then, before withdrawing, he placed a lingering palm on my cheek — a gesture that completely threw me off and left me feeling shaken and overcome with emotion. It had caught me by surprise. I wanted us to kiss. *Just kiss me, will you, if only to help me get over being so visibly flustered.*

I watched him pivot and walk away.

You don't do that and walk away, I thought, *and so stiffly too.* I wanted him to bring his other palm to my cheek and hold my face, hold my face and let me be the younger of the two, and then kiss me deep in the mouth. It felt as though we'd just been in bed together and he'd stopped talking to me and then simply vanished.

The feeling stayed with me all night, and I kept waking in fits and starts. The night was still young and we could easily have gone elsewhere for another drink. I could have rushed after him and asked to offer him something at a café nearby — just to be together and not say goodbye so soon. Yet something held me back and eventually another voice in me reminded me that I was not exactly displeased by how the evening had turned out on the end of a long, dull Sunday when nothing remotely like this was planned. Perhaps he'd seen that sometimes it's best to stop things when they're perfect rather than race on and watch them sour.

I walked my bike on this lovely November night: the deserted glinting cobblestones, the Brassaï effect we'd discussed, my clumsy kiss under his ears, and the matter about being almost half his age, all these buoyed my spirit and made me feel quite happy. Perhaps he'd understood things better than I ever could; and if he understood, then he knew something I was barely beginning to realize myself: that perhaps I wasn't ready, any more than he was, not tonight, not tomorrow night, not even next week, which was when it finally dawned on me that he might not attend next Sunday's concert, not because he didn't want to but because he already sensed that, at the last minute next Sunday evening, I'd be the one who'd find a reason not to show up.

Two evenings later, I was just finishing a master class devoted to the last movement of Beethoven's D Minor sonata when suddenly, at the door, there he was, standing with his hands in the pockets of his blue blazer, looking a touch gawky for such an elegant man, and yet not in the slightest bit uncomfortable. He held the door for the six or seven who were starting to leave the hall, and seeing they were filing out without holding the door or thanking him, he smiled broadly at them, finally thanking them for the tip. I must have been beaming. What a lovely way to surprise someone.

"You're not displeased then?"

I shook my head. *Like you needed to ask.*

"What were you planning after class?"

"I usually have coffee or a juice somewhere."

"Mind if I join?"

"Mind if I join?" I mimicked.

I took him to my favorite café where I go after teaching and where sometimes a colleague or a student joins me as we sit and watch people race along the sidewalks at this time of day — people on last-minute errands, others looking to put off heading home and shutting their door to the world, and then some just rushing from one corner of their lives to another. The tables around us were all filled with people, and for some reason that I've never been able to define, I like when everyone seems bunched together, almost elbow to elbow with strangers. "Are you really not displeased I came then?" he asked again. I smiled and shook my head. I told him I was still not recovered from the surprise.

"Good surprise, then?"

"Very good surprise."

"If I didn't find you at the conservatory," he said, "I was going to try every luxury hotel with a piano bar. Very simple."

"It would have taken you a long time."

"I gave myself forty days and forty nights, and then I would have tried the conservatory. Instead I tried the conservatory first."

"But weren't we planning on meeting this coming Sunday?"

"I wasn't too sure."

That I didn't object or say anything to gainsay his assumption must have confirmed his suspicion. Indeed, our silence regarding next Sunday's concert made us smile uneasily. "I have wonderful memories of last Sunday," I ended up saying. "So do I," he replied.

"Who was the lovely pianist with whom you were playing?" he asked.

"She's a very talented third-year student from Thailand, very, very gifted."

"The way you looked at each other while

playing clearly suggests there is more than just teacher-pupil affinity between you."

"Yes, she came all the way here to study with me." I could tell where he was leading and shook my head with mock reproof at the insinuation.

"And may I ask what you're doing later?"

Bold, I thought.

"You mean tonight? Nothing."

"Doesn't someone like you have a friend, a partner, someone special?"

"Someone like me?" Were we really going to repeat last Sunday's conversation?

"I meant young, sparkling, clearly fascinating, to say nothing of very handsome."

"There is no one," I said, then looked away.

Was I really trying to cut him off? Or was I enjoying this without wanting to show it?

"You don't take compliments well, do you?"

I looked at him and shook my head again, but without humor this time.

"So no one, no one?" he finally asked.

"Nobody."

"Not even the occasional . . . ?"

"I don't do the occasional."

"Never?" he asked, almost baffled.

"Never."

But I could hear my tone stiffen. He was

trying to be playful, prodding, borderline flirtatious, and here I was coming off as mirthless, dour, and, worst of all, self-righteous.

"But there must have been someone special?"

"There was."

"Why did it end?"

"We were friends, then we were lovers, then she split. But we stayed friends."

"Was there ever a he in your life?"

"Yes."

"How did it end?"

"He got married."

"Ah, the marriage canard!"

"I thought so too at the time. But they've been together for years now. They were together before he started with me."

At first, he didn't say anything but he seemed to question the whole setup. "Did the two of you remain friends?"

I wasn't sure I wanted him to ask, yet I loved being asked.

"We haven't spoken in ages, and I don't know that we're friends, though I'm sure we will always be. He's always read me extremely well, and I have a feeling that he suspects that if I never write it's not because I don't care but because a part of me still does and always will, just as I know he still cares, which is why he too never writes. And knowing this is good enough for me."

"Even though he's the one who got married?"

"Even though he's the one who got married," I echoed. "And besides," I added, as though it dispelled any ambiguity, "he teaches in the US, and I'm here in Paris — kind of settles it, doesn't it? Unseen but always there."

"Doesn't settle it at all. Why haven't you gone after him, even if he is married? Why give up so easily?"

The near-critical tone in his voice was hard to miss. Why was he reproaching me? Was he not interested then?

"Besides, how long ago was it?" he asked.

I knew my answer would leave him totally stumped. "Fifteen years."

Suddenly, he stopped asking and went silent. As I expected, he had not figured that so many years could go by and leave me still attached to someone who had become an invisible presence.

"It belongs to the past," I said, trying to make amends.

"Nothing belongs to the past." But then he right away asked: "You still think of him, don't you?"

I nodded because I did not want to say yes.

"Do you miss him?"

"When I am alone — sometimes, yes. But it doesn't intrude, doesn't make me sad. I can go entire weeks without thinking of him. Sometimes I want to tell him things, but then I put it off, and even telling myself that I'm putting it off gives me some pleasure, though we may never speak. He taught me everything. My father said there were no taboos in bed; my lover helped me cast them off. He was my first."

Michel shook his head with a confiding smile that reassured me. "How many after him?" he asked.

"Not many. All short-lived. Men and women."

"Why?"

"Maybe because I never really let go or lose myself with others. After an instant of passion, I always fall back to being the autonomous me."

He took a last sip of his coffee.

"At some point in your life you will need to call him. The moment will come. It always does. But perhaps I shouldn't be saying all this."

"Why?" I asked.

"Oh, you know why."

I liked what he'd just said, but it left us both silent. "The autonomous you, then," he finally said, obviously eliding what had just transpired between us that very second. "Difficult, aren't you?"

"My father used to say so as well, because I could never decide on anything, what to do in life, where to live, what to study, whom to love. Stick to music, he said. Sooner or later, the rest would come. He started his career at the age of thirty-two — so I still have some time, though not much, if I'm to time myself to his clock. We've been exceptionally close, ever since I was a baby. He was a philologist and writing his dissertation at home while my mother was a therapist in a hospital, so he was the one in charge of diapers and all the rest. We had help but I was always with him. He's the one who taught me to love music — ironically, the very same piece I was teaching when you walked in this afternoon. When I teach it I still hear his voice."

"My father too taught me music. I was just a bad student."

I liked this sudden convergence of co-incidences though I was reluctant to make too much of it either. He kept staring at me without saying anything. But then he said something that caught me off guard once again: "You are so handsome." It had come totally unprompted, so that rather than react to his words, I tried to change the subject, except that in doing so I heard myself mutter something more unprompted yet. "You make me nervous."

"What makes you say that?"

"I don't know. Maybe because I don't really know what you're after, or where you'd want me to stop and not go further."

"Should be very clear by now. If anything I'm the one who should be nervous."

"Why?"

"Because I'm probably just a whim for you, or maybe a few rungs higher than an occasional."

I scoffed at this.

"And by the way" — I hesitated before saying it but felt impelled to say it — "I'm not very good at beginnings."

He chuckled. "Was this thrown in for my benefit?"

"Maybe."

"Well, but to come back to what I was saying: You are unbelievably handsome. And the problem is either that you know it and are aware of its power over others or that you need to pretend not to — which makes you not just difficult to decipher but, for someone like me, dangerous."

189

All I did was nod listlessly. I didn't want him to feel that what he'd just told me was misplaced. So I stared at him, smiled, and in another setting would have touched his eyelids before kissing them both.

As it got darker, the lights of our café and of the adjoining one were lit. They cast a luminous, unsteady glow on his features, and for the first time, I was aware of his lips, his forehead, and his eyes. *He's* the handsome one, I thought. I should have said so, and the moment was ripe for it. But I kept quiet. I did not want to echo his own words; it would have sounded like a strained and contrived attempt to establish parity between us. But I did love his eyes. And he was still staring at me.

"You remind me of my son," he finally said.

"Do we look alike?"

"No, but you're the same age. He too loves classical music. So I used to take him to the Sunday-evening concerts, the way my father had so often done with me."

"Do you still go together?"

"No. He lives in Sweden, mostly."

"But the two of you are close?"

"I wish. My divorce with his mother ruined things between us, though I'm sure she did nothing to hurt our relationship.

190

But he knew about me of course and, I suppose, never forgave me. Or he used it as an excuse to turn against me, which he'd been wanting to do since his early twenties, God knows why."

"How did they find out?"

"She did first. One early evening she walked in and found me listening to slow jazz and nursing a drink. I was alone and just by watching me and the look on my face she knew right away that I was in love. Classic feminine intuition! She put down her handbag by the coffee table, sat next to me on the sofa, and even reached out and had a sip of my drink: 'Is she someone I know?' she asked after a long, long silence. I knew exactly what she meant and there was no point denying it. 'It's not a she,' I replied. 'Ah,' she said. I still remember the last remnants of sunlight on the carpet and against the furniture, the smoky smell of my whiskey, and the cat lying next to me. Sunlight, when I see it in my living room, still reminds me of that conversation. 'So it's worse than I thought,' she said. 'Why?' I asked. 'Because against a woman I still stand a chance, but against who you are, there's nothing I can do. I cannot change you.' Thus ended almost twenty years of marriage. My son was bound to find out soon enough, and he did."

"How?"

"*I* told him. I was under the illusion that he'd understand. He didn't."

"I'm sorry" was all I could say.

He shrugged his shoulders. "I don't regret the turn in my life. But I do regret losing him. He never calls when he is in Paris, seldom even writes, and doesn't pick up when I call."

He looked at his watch. Was it time to go already?

"So it's not a mistake that I tracked you down?" he asked for the third time, perhaps because he loved hearing me say that it absolutely wasn't, which I enjoyed telling him.

"Not a mistake."

"And you weren't upset with me about the other evening?" he asked.

I knew exactly what he was referring to.

"Maybe I was — a bit."

He smiled. I could tell he was eager to leave the café, so I moved closer to him, my shoulder touching his. Which was when he put his arm around me and drew me to him, almost urging me to rest my head on his shoulder. I didn't know whether this was meant to reassure me or simply humor a young man who had opened up and spoken some touching words to an older man. Perhaps it was the prelude to a goodbye hug. So, fearing the unavoidable leave-taking, I blurted out, "I'm not doing anything tonight."

"Yes, I know. You told me."

But he must have sensed that I was nervous or that his tone was off.

"You are an amazing and —" He didn't finish his sentence.

He was about to pay but I stopped his hand. Then as I held it I stared at it.

"What are you doing?" he asked almost reproachfully.

"Paying."

"No, you were staring at my hand."

"I wasn't," I protested. But I had stared at his hand.

"It's called age," he said. Then a moment later: "Haven't changed your mind, have you?" He bit his lower lip but then right away released it. He was waiting for my answer.

And then because there was nothing I could think of saying to him but still felt the need to say something, anything, "Let's not say goodbye, not just yet." But I realized that this could easily be viewed as a request to extend our time together by a short while in the café, so I decided to opt for something bolder. "Don't let me go home tonight, Michel," I said. I know I blushed saying this, and was already scrambling for ways to apologize and take back my words when he came to my rescue.

"I was struggling to ask the very same thing but, once again, you beat me to it. The truth is," he went on, "I don't do this frequently. Actually, I haven't done this in a long time."

"This?" I said, with a slight jeer in my voice.

"This."

We left shortly after. We must have walked with my bike a good twenty or thirty minutes to his home. He offered to hail a taxi. I said no, that I preferred to walk; besides, the bike was not the easiest thing to fold, and taxi drivers always complained. "I love your bike. I love that you have such a bike." Then, catching himself: "I'm speaking nonsense, aren't I?" We were walking side by side with hardly a foot's distance between us and our hands kept grazing. Then I reached for his and held it for a few moments. This would break the ice, I thought. But he kept quiet. A few more paces on the cobbled street, and I let go of his hand.

"I do love this," I said.

"This?" he teased. "Meaning the Brassaï

effect?" he asked.

"No, me and you. It's what we should have done two nights ago."

He looked down at the sidewalk, smiling. Was I perhaps rushing things? I liked how our walk tonight was a repeat of the other evening. The crowd and the singing on the bridge, the glinting slate cobbles, the bike with its strapped bag I would eventually lock to a pole, and his passing comment about wishing to buy one just like it.

What never ceased to amaze me and cast a halo around our evening was that ever since we'd met, we'd been thinking along the same lines, and when we feared we weren't or felt we were wrong-footing each other, it was simply because we had learned not to trust that anyone could possibly think and behave the way we did, which was why I was so diffident with him and mistrusted every impulse in myself and couldn't have been happier when I saw how easily we'd shed some of our screens. How wonderful to have finally said exactly what was on my mind ever since Sunday: *Don't let me go home tonight.* How wonderful that he'd seen through my blushing on Sunday night and made me want to admit I'd blushed, only then to concede that he himself had blushed as well. Could two people who'd basically spent less than four hours together still have so few secrets from each other? I wondered what the guilty secret was that I held in my vault of craven falsehoods.

"I lied about the occasionals," I said.

"I figured as much," he replied, almost discounting the struggle behind my avowal.

When we finally stepped into one of those tight, small Parisian elevators with no space between us, "Now will you hold me?" I asked. He shut the slim elevator doors and pressed the button to his floor. I heard the loud clank of the engine and the strain as the elevator began its ascent, when suddenly he didn't just hold me but cupped my face in both his hands and kissed me deep on the mouth. I shut my eyes and kissed him back. I'd been waiting for this for such a long time. All I remember hearing was the sound of the very old elevator grinding and staggering its way up to his floor as I kept hoping the sound would never end and the elevator never stop.

Then, once he closed the door of his apartment, it was my turn to kiss him, just as he had kissed me. I knew he was taller, and I sensed he was stronger. I just wanted him to know that I was holding nothing back and wasn't going to.

"Perhaps what we need is a good drink,"

he said. "I have some wonderful single malts. It is single malts you like, correct?"

The question about drinks caught me totally off guard, especially as I was just about to drop my backpack and remove my coat and sweater and ask him to hold me again. My heart was racing, yet suddenly I felt awkward, even if none of this was unfamiliar to me. I kept wanting him to stop moving around so much. But I said nothing and took my time removing my backpack and placing it on an armchair.

"Do you want to remove your coat?" he asked.

"In a while," I said.

"I like your backpack," he said, turning around.

"It was a gift. A friend" — and because there was hesitation on his face — "just a friend."

He pointed to the sofa for me to sit and said he was bringing in the glasses. So I sat down. I don't know why but I suddenly felt cold, so I stood up again while he was in the foyer and leaned against the radiator. Feeling the warmth inadequate, I placed my arms against it as well.

"Are you feeling all right?"

"Yes, just cold," I said. I was almost not going to tell him that I was suddenly close to freezing.

"I'll shut the window, then." And he did.

Did I want ice in my whiskey?

I shook my head.

But I didn't move away from the radiator and continued to keep both hands and the front of my body glued to it. He put down the glasses on the coffee table, approached me from behind and began massaging my shoulders. I loved the way he kneaded my neck and shoulder blades.

"Better?" he asked.

"More," I said. Then without knowing why: "I told you I get nervous."

"Because of me?"

I hunched my shoulders, knowing he'd understand I meant *I don't know, maybe it's not you, or the evening, who knows, just don't stop.*

He had strong hands — and he knew, just as I wanted him to know — that I was yielding bit by bit each time he pressed the area right under my skull and sent the most stirring shudder all the way down my spine. When he was done, he put his arms around me and pressed his chest to my back, both his hands clasping my stomach. I wouldn't have minded had he gone lower, but he didn't, though I knew it had crossed his mind, because I sensed a millisecond of hesitation. Gently, he drew me to the sofa.

But then he started with the whiskey, poured some into both our glasses, suddenly remembered something and rushed to the kitchen, coming back with two bowls, one with nuts, the other with mini salted biscuits. He sat down at the other end of the sofa, we clinked our glasses, uttered a toast, and took our first sip. He wanted to know what I thought. I didn't know what I thought. So I said I was still quite new to single malts but that I liked them. He offered the bowl of nuts, watched me take some, then placed it back on the coffee table without helping himself to any. I took a second sip and told him that I was still cold. "Could I have a cup of tea instead?" What kind of tea did I want, he had so many, he said. Any tea, I replied, just something hot. On his way to the kitchen he touched my cheek and the side of my neck. It reminded me of my mother when I wasn't feeling well and she'd check to see if I had a fever. But his was not a fever touch, and I smiled. Within minutes, immediately following the beep of the microwave oven, he was back and I was cupping a warm mug in both hands. "So much better," I said, almost laughing at how happy the tea made me feel.

Once again he stood up, and put on some music.

I listened for a moment. "Brazilian?"

"Correct." He seemed very pleased with himself. He had bought the CD the day before, he said.

By my smile, he knew I'd inferred the reason for the purchase.

Did I understand Portuguese, he asked.

Some, did he?

Not a word.

It made us laugh. We were both nervous.

We talked mostly about old partners. His had been an architect who eventually moved to Montreal years ago. "Yours?" he asked. "And I don't mean the marriage canard." So he did remember the man who'd got away and thrown my life off course. I told him that my longest relationship was with a kid I'd known in elementary school whom I met almost fifteen years later in a gay bar on the seedy outskirts of Rome. What astounded me was that he confessed to having a crush on me when we were eight. I told him I'd been totally fascinated by him when I was nine. Why hadn't he said anything? Why hadn't I? Why hadn't either of us known about ourselves? All we wanted to do was make up for lost time. I think we could not believe how lucky we were to have reconnected.

"How long were you together?"

"Less than two years."

"Why did you separate?"

"I used to think it was good old ordinary domesticity that killed what we had. But it was more than that. He wanted to adopt a child, he even wanted me to father the child. What he wanted was a family."

"And you didn't?"

"I don't know that I didn't. I just knew that I wasn't ready, I was entirely devoted to music and still am. The real truth is, I couldn't wait to live alone again."

He gave me a quizzical look: "Is this by any chance meant as a warning to me?" he asked.

"I don't know." I smiled to cover up my embarrassment. His question was totally premature. But then, in his place, I would have asked the same thing.

"Perhaps I shouldn't have said anything, but I'm looking at all this from the other end. Age. I'm sure it's crossed your mind more than once."

"Age is no problem."

"Isn't it?"

"I told you so on Sunday. How quickly we forget."

"I don't remember."

"You're losing your memory."

"I was flustered."

"And I wasn't?"

"I've thought of you ever since we said good night outside the brasserie. I went to bed thinking of you, woke up thinking of you, and was in a trance all of Monday, basically kicking myself. I can't even bring myself to believe you're sitting under my roof."

He stopped speaking, looked at me, and just said, "And I want to kiss you."

I was more surprised this time than when we kissed on stepping into the elevator. It made me feel we had never kissed before and that the shadow of uneasiness while walking home with him without being able to hold hands had not been dispelled. He put down his glass, moved over to me, and kissed me lightly on the lips, almost diffidently, while, like the obliging soundtrack to our earlier kiss, I kept hearing behind the faint Brazilian singer playing in our room the sound of the elevator coming down to remind me that kissing to the sound of an old elevator going up and down the stairwell was like kissing under the patter of falling rain on a rooftop in the country, and that I liked the sound and didn't want it to end because I felt snug, protected, and safe under its spell, because, without intruding on us, it gave a voice to the world outside his living room and reminded me that all this was not just happening in my mind. What he was really asking perhaps was for us to take our time and not hurry, and, if need be, backtrack if things went faster than either of us wanted. This I had never done before. Then he kissed me a second time, also lightly.

"Feeling better?" he asked.

"Much. Just hold me again, please." I wanted to be held and to wrap my arms around him. I liked the texture of his sweater on my face, the smell of wool, and, behind the wool around his underarms, a faint scent that could only have been his body's.

So I whispered the words of the song in Portuguese:

De que serve ter o mapa se o fim está
  traçado
De que serve a terra à vista se o barco
  está parado
De que serve ter a chave se a porta está
  aberta

"Translate," he said.

What good is the map if the end's already
known?
What good is landfall if the boat stalls?
What good is a key if the door's wide
open?

He loved this, he said, and asked me to
repeat the words, which I did.

Soon, he said, "Let's lie down." He
showed me to the bedroom. I was about to
unbutton my shirt, but "Don't," he said,
"let me do it." I wanted to be naked before
him but didn't know how to say this. So I
let him unbutton my shirt without touching
any of his clothing. He didn't seem to mind.
"It's because" — and he hesitated — "I
want this to be very special," he said.

And as we lay down, we embraced and
sought each other's mouths. But I could
sense we were still unsteady and off-balance.
Something was missing. It was not passion
we lacked; it was conviction. Had we,
perhaps, slowed things down to a halt? Had
I failed him? Were we changing our minds?
He must have felt it as well; it's something
no one can conceal or fail to pick up. He
stared at me and all he said was, "Will you
let me make you happy, just let me, I so
want to."

"Do anything you want. You make me

happy as it is."

Hearing this he could not wait and kissed me again and began to finish unbuttoning my shirt. "Mind if I take your shirt off?" *What a question,* I thought as I nodded. Then, as he helped me: "I love your skin, I love your chest, your shoulders, your smell. Are you still cold?" he asked, all the while gently caressing my chest.

"No," I said, "not any longer."

Then, once again he surprised me: "I'd love us to take a hot shower."

I must have looked at him with totally baffled eyes. "Why not, if you want to."

We stood up, and stepped into his bathroom. It was larger than my entire living room.

I couldn't believe the number of bottles lining the floor of his large, enclosed glass shower. "Two for you, two for me," he said, producing four folded navy towels. In an effort to bring some humor to the situation as we were getting undressed and already touching, I asked if they served breakfast here in the morning. "And how," he replied. "A complimentary breakfast is included for all hotel guests." We were naked and hard when we kissed again.

"Shut your eyes and trust me," he said. "I want to make you happy." I didn't know what he was up to but I did as he asked. I heard him grab a cloth, and I immediately recognized the scent of the shower gel, because it smelled of chamomile, which reminded me of my parents' home and, despite the weather outside tonight, it took me right back to our summers in Italy, which made me feel at home in this home that wasn't my home. He began to rub my body, and I let myself go with the feeling. "Don't open your eyes," he cautioned as he palmed my face gently with soap and then asked if he could shampoo my hair, to which I said of course he could, and while the shampoo sat on my hair after he'd rubbed it in, I heard him wash himself, only then to feel his fingers rubbing and prodding my skull time and time again. "Don't cheat and look," he said, and I could tell from his voice that he was smiling, almost laughing at what the two of us were doing in the shower.

After the shower, and while my eyes were still shut, he opened the glass door and helped me step out slowly, then insisted on drying my body, my hair, my back, and underarms, and then walked me to the bedroom and asked me to lie on his bed. I loved knowing I was naked and being stared at, loved being coddled this way, loved when he started rubbing a lotion on me that felt wonderful each time he poured more of it on his palm and touched me everywhere. I felt like a toddler being washed and dried by his parent, which also took me back to my very earliest childhood when my father would shower with me in his arms. I must have been one or so — why was all this coming to me now, and why did it suddenly release me from a box whose lid had been depriving me of air and of light and sound and of the scent of flowers and herbs in the summertime? Why was I being pulled out of myself as though I'd been a prisoner whose jailer happened to be none other than myself and me alone? And what was this product that I'd never felt on my skin before? What did I want from this man and what was I going to give him in return? Was he doing all this because I'd told him I was nervous, because I'd warned him I found beginnings difficult? I let him do as he pleased, because I liked it so much and felt so desirable that I desired him even more in return, more than I'd done the moment I'd seen him in church and held back from embracing his chest. I thought I knew what he was about to do, but what he did next, once again, came as a complete surprise, so that when he finally asked me to open my eyes and look straight into his, I was entirely all his and when he kissed me again and again I didn't need to say or think of anything, I didn't need to do a thing except give myself over to someone who seemed to know me, and know my body and what it craved far better than I did, because he must have known it the moment he'd spoken to me in church and I'd touched his hand, known when he'd asked me to wait for him outside the church and then invited me to dinner, known when he stopped short of where we might have been headed that night and abruptly said good night, known everything about me when he saw me blush so easily and then pushed the matter just a tad farther to see how I'd react, known that I'd lost my soul for so long and was now finding I'd owned it all along but didn't know where to look for it or how to find it without him — *Lost my soul, lost my soul,* I wanted to say, and then heard myself mutter the words, *Lost my soul, all these years.* "Don't," he said, as though fearing I was on the point of tears. "Just say I'm not hurting you," he said. I nodded. "No, say, 'You're not hurting me,' say it because you mean it." "You're not hurting me," I said. "Say it again, say it many times." And I said, "You're not hurting me," because I meant it, "you're not hurting me, you're not hurting me, you're not, you're not," and then realized that even as I spoke these words more times than he had asked, that what he'd also done was help me leave behind — everything I had brought with me that night, my thoughts, my music, my dreams, my name, my loves, my scruples, my bike, everything else was dumped on my jacket and my backpack in the living room or stuffed into the bag that was strapped to my bike that was locked to a signpost that was all the way downstairs before we'd taken the elevator, which once again, now when we were making love, gave out its telltale squeal, because who knows which tenant in the building had pressed a button to call the elevator downstairs and would soon step inside, click shut the slim doors behind him, and ride his wobbly way up to who knows which floor, and I didn't care what floor that was, because if I thought these muddled thoughts it was because I was trying and failing each time to think that I wasn't losing my grip when I knew damn well that I was just desperately holding on to mere slivers of reality and feeling them slip from me, and feeling ecstatic each time they did, because I loved that he was seeing this happen to me, and I wanted him to see this on my face even while he was doing the most generous thing in the world, which was to wait and still wait while I kept repeating he wasn't hurting me, wasn't hurting me, just as he'd asked me to, until I caught myself begging him not to wait, because this was the polite thing to ask, hoping he'd decide for me as well, because by now his body knew mine better than it knew itself.

There'd been only a very short awkward hiccup in what had been a moment of perfect intimacy between two men who until then hadn't seen each other naked. It had happened in the shower when he was holding my penis and my eyes were shut because of the soap. "I don't know how to ask this," he had said, "but —" And then he hesitated again.

"Yes?" He was making *me* nervous now and I couldn't even open my eyes.

"Are you Jewish?" he finally asked.

"Seriously?" I replied, almost laughing. "Can't you tell?"

"I was trying to base my guess on other facts besides the obvious."

"The obvious says it pretty loudly. How many Jews or Muslims have you seen naked?"

"None," he replied. "You are my very first."

His sudden candor aroused me even more, which was why I pressed his body against mine.

"Fabiola," he explained right after we were jolted from sleep by the sound of the service door banging. "She always lets the wind slam it shut." When I looked at my watch it was already past eight a.m. and I had to teach at eleven. But I felt very lazy. He, however, had already released me from his embrace and was sitting up, while his feet, I thought, kept searching for his slippers.

"Come back to bed," I said.

"What, more?" he asked, feigning shock. I had loved being held in his arms with my back turned to him and his breath on my neck. I wasn't holding back.

There had been a moment of hesitation just after we'd made love that night when I felt it was time to get dressed to leave. "You're not getting out of bed, are you?" he had asked.

"Bathroom," I said.

I was lying.

"Not leaving though."

"Not leaving." But I was lying here as well. I had meant to leave, even if I'd be doing it out of habit. I was going to explain that I always leave after sex, either because I want to or because I sense my host can't wait to see me gone, because I myself almost always want to see occasionals out the door afterward. *Hurry up with the socks, stuff them in your pockets if you have to, just go.* I'd even mastered the art of the civil if totally perfunctory way of delaying my hasty exit, the way a host may sometimes feign reluctance to see you turn down a glass of water or a bite of something while you're racing out from his world, from his things, from the smell of his hair, his sheets, his towels. Here the matter was slightly odd, and I didn't say anything. I didn't really want to get out of bed but didn't know how to read, much less trust the look of surprise on his face. And yet, as I'd noticed from the time we were walking to his apartment and relishing how our hands kept nearing yet missing each other, this hadn't exactly been slam-dunk sex either.

After we made love that night he said we should head out to grab a bite to eat. "I'm starving." "Me too," I echoed. "But we should hurry." Neither of us had realized that it was past midnight. "Do we look like we've been fucking?" "Yes," I said. "Maybe people will know." "I want them to know."

"So do I."

We had dinner in a small but noisy place that tended to stay open late. The waiters knew him there, and some of the regulars knew him as well. It gave the two of us a shared thrill to sense they suspected what we'd been up to not fifteen minutes earlier.

"I want one more hug," I said that morning.

"Just a hug?"

Before I knew it, I had my legs wrapped tight around his waist.

"And so may I ask you something?" he said, his face no more than an inch away from mine, with one palm on my forehead brushing my hair away from my eyes.

I had no idea what he had in mind — perhaps, I figured, something to do with our bodies or something a touch awkward, about performance, or would it be about protection?

"Are you busy this evening?"

The question almost made me laugh. "Totally free," I said.

"Then how about our little bistro?"

"What time?"

"Nine?"

I nodded.

I had forgotten the precise address of the

place. He named the street. Then, while trying not to sound too self-important, he said they sometimes kept a free table for him there. "I frequently bring clients there for lunch or dinner."

"And others?"

He smiled.

"If you only knew."

The maid must have been told he had a guest — probably while I was in the shower — because when he showed me to the dining room, breakfast was served for two. Coffee and a host of wonderful things, breads, cheeses, and jams that seemed homemade. He said he liked quince jam and fig jam. Most people liked berries and marmalades. "But suit yourself."

He had to rush to his office. "Nine then?"

We left together. I told him I was going to ride home to change and then head to the conservatory, after which I had a lunch scheduled with a colleague. I don't know why I provided so much information about my day. He listened, he watched me unlock the bike, admired its frame again, told me to fold it and bring it inside the next time, then he stood there, and, unlike the first time, watched as I rode away.

But it was still too early in the day. So I rode down one street and then another, crossed the bridge, not caring where I was headed, eager to find a bakery where I might stop, sit, have another cup of coffee and think of him, I didn't want the events of the morning to brush away the feeling or the memory of last night, of how we kissed savagely in the end while all I liked hearing was the silence and the comforting wheezing of the old elevator going up and down reminding me each time that we were no longer the last who'd used it.

Usually, I forget, or try to put away what happened at night, which isn't difficult since things seldom last more than an hour or two. Sometimes it's as though it hadn't occurred at all, and I'm happy not to remember.

Sitting down on this very clear morning, I liked watching all these people headed to work while feeling I was on an extended Christmas Day. The sex had had nothing unusual about it, but I liked how he had paid attention to everything, from the moment he handed me the towels to the way he cared for my body, my pleasure, mindful of everything, and always so tactful and kind, with something verging on deference for the young body that was half his age. Even the way he'd kept rubbing and caressing my hand and then my wrist, asking for trust and little else when my eyes were shut, just rubbing my wrists, which he held down gently on the bed, the kindest gesture known to man. Why had no one ever held my wrists that way and brought me so much joy with such minute and seemingly insignificant caresses? If he forgot, I would ask him to rub my wrists just as he'd done before.

I put down the paper and without thinking had raised the collar of my fleece jacket and felt it rub my face. It reminded me of his unshaven cheek this morning, when we'd made love again. I wanted my coat to smell of him. What aftershave did he wear? It was so faint, but I wanted to know. I would learn to rub his cheek with mine tomorrow morning.

And then I thought of my father who said he'd be in Paris for Christmas in a few weeks. I wondered if Michel and I would still be together by then. I wanted my father to meet him and wondered what he'd think of him. He and Miranda had promised to bring along the boy this time — it was time I saw my younger brother again, he said. I would take them to my café here, and if Michel were still a presence in my life, Miranda and I would simply sit back and watch both men figure out who was the younger of the two.

I spent the rest of the day in a mild daze. Three students plus a lecture prepared fifteen minutes before class. At lunch all I kept thinking of was dinner that night, the single malts, the nuts and salted biscuits, and the moment when he'd once again offer two towels for me and two for him. Would he be as hospitable tonight or would he have changed into someone I didn't know? I hoped my best shirt was well pressed, and, when I checked, I found it was. I had a mind to put on a tie but decided against it. I combed my hair but I couldn't wait for him to brush my forehead with his hand. Then on my way out, I ran to my local cobbler to have my shoes shined.

I think I'm happy. That's what I was going to say to him. *I think I'm happy.* I knew I should avoid saying this on our third evening, but I didn't care. I wanted to say it.

When I arrived at the restaurant that night I didn't find him and realized to my extreme embarrassment that I didn't know his surname. It left me feeling completely flustered. I would never dare say that I had come to meet Michel or Monsieur Michel. But before I had a chance to utter something that was bound to mortify me, one of the waiters recognized me and right away took me to what had been our table three nights earlier. It occurred to me that, despite Michel's denial, I was not the first young man to have walked into the brasserie looking slightly awkward and whom the help had been trained to spot as yet another of his guests. I was a touch miffed, but decided not to nurse a grudge or let the feeling fester. Perhaps I was making it all up. And maybe I was, because when I was shown to his table not five steps away from the door, there he was, already seated, nursing an aperitif. In my confused state I'd failed to notice he'd been staring at me all along.

We hugged. And then, unable to control myself, I told him, "I've spent the most wonderful day of the year."

"Why?" he asked.

"I still haven't figured out why," I said, "but it may have something to do with last night."

"Last night *and* this morning for me." He smiled. I liked that he wasn't reluctant to show he had appreciated our hasty little morning sequel. I liked his mood, his smile, liked everything. A moment of silence and I couldn't hold back: "You're wonderful, I've been meaning to tell you, you're just wonderful!"

As soon as I unfolded my napkin, it hit me. I had lost my appetite. "I'm not at all hungry," I said.

"Now you're the one who is wonderful."

"Why?"

"Because I'm not hungry either but I wasn't going to say it. Let's just go home. Maybe a snack. A single malt?"

"A single malt. With nuts and salted things?"

"Definitely nuts and salted things."

He turned to the headwaiter: "Apologies to the chef, but we've changed our mind. À demain."

When we reached his home, we ditched the idea of a drink or a snack. We took off our clothes, left them on the floor, skipped the shower, and went straight to bed.

Thursday that week we met again at nine at the same restaurant.

Friday for lunch.

And then for dinner as well.

After breakfast that Saturday, he said he was going to drive to the country and that I was welcome to join him — *if I was free,* he added with that guarded and typically unassuming, ironic lilt in his voice meant to show he was perfectly prepared to accept I had a life outside of our meetings and that he was never going to ask why, where, when, or with whom. But having spoken, he probably felt he might as well go all the way:

"We could come back on Sunday evening just in time for our one-week anniversary concert." I couldn't tell what was making him slightly uneasy, the invitation to spend the weekend with him or the open admission that the two of us already had an anniversary to celebrate. To tidy things with his usual reserve he quickly added that, if I wished to join him, he could drop me at my flat, wait in the car while I packed a few warm things — it gets cold at night — and we'd be off.

"Where to?" I asked, which was my hasty way of saying, *Of course I'll come.*

"I have a home about an hour away from the city."

I joked and said I felt like Cinderella.

"How so?"

"When does the clock strike midnight? When does the honeymoon end?" I asked.

"It ends when it ends."

"Is there an expiration date?"

"The manufacturers haven't determined an expiration yet. So we're on our own. And besides, this is different," he said.

"Don't you say this to everyone?"

"I do. And I have. But you and I have something very special, and for me totally unusual. If you'll let me, I hope to prove it to you this weekend."

"A likely story," I said. We both laughed.

"The irony is that I may even succeed in proving it — and then where will we be?" He looked at me. "And that — if you care to know — is the part that scares me more than a little."

I could have asked him to elaborate, but, once again, felt that this could lead into territory neither of us wished to enter.

The home, when we finally reached it more than an hour later, wasn't Brideshead but it wasn't Howards End either. "I grew up here," he said. "It's big, it's old, and it's always, always cold. Even the bikes are old and rickety, nothing like yours. There's a lake down beyond the wood and I like it there. It's where I recharge. I'll show you around later. Plus there's an old Steinway."

"Great. But is it tuned?"

He looked slightly embarrassed. "I had it tuned."

"When, though?"

"Yesterday."

"For no reason, I suppose."

"For no reason."

We both smiled. It was moments of sudden and radiant intimacy like these that made me want to shout, *It's been years since I've been like this with anyone.*

I put my arm around his shoulder. "So

you knew I'd come."

"Not knew. Hoped."

He showed me around the house, then walked me to the large parlor.

We didn't exactly step inside but stood at the doorway like two characters looking on as Velázquez paints his two monarchs. The ageless wooden floor around the large Persian rugs was gleaming gold and was clearly the beneficiary of years of buffing. One could smell the wax polish. "I'll always remember," said Michel, "how it used to get so lonely in the fall at the start of each school year when we'd come to spend weekends here. Those days felt like never-ending rainy Sundays that start at nine in the morning and never let up until winter comes and we'd be driving back to Paris by four feeling sapped and silent in the car. My parents hated each other but never said it. The only thing that stirred any joy — and it was more relief than joy — was Sunday evening when we'd unlock the door to our flat in town, turn on one light after the other, until life seemed to pick up its pace with the promise of a concert, which was when my whole world rose from its induced stupor called schoolwork, called dinner, called Mother, called silence and loneliness, and, worst of all, perpetual boyhood. I wouldn't wish my childhood or adolescence in this house on anyone. Life was like a waiting room at a doctor's office and my turn never came."

He saw me smile. "All I ever did here was homework and masturbate. I think there isn't a room in this whole mansion where I didn't do homework."

"And masturbate."

It made us both laugh.

We were having a simple, almost frugal lunch in the dining room. From what I inferred, he normally drove here late on Saturday mornings and would leave by Sunday afternoon. "Habit," he explained.

The L-shaped house was large, and its façade was late-eighteenth-century Palladian: very plain and unassuming, almost bland in its predictable symmetries, which probably explained its restrained yet welcoming grace. And then came the mysterious right-angle wing, which created an intimate space that yielded a well-tended, semi-enclosed Italian garden. The mansard roof with its dormer windows immediately made me think of a cold room up there where the lonely boy who would one day become my lover sat at his desk and dutifully did his homework while nursing all manner of lurid thoughts. I felt for the boy.

His mother always made him bring his homework along; so there was little else to do here, much less to enjoy, he said.

I asked him about his school days. He'd attended the Lycée J. "I hated it," he said, "but my father would sometimes drop by and arrange to take me out for a few hours. It was to be our secret. He too had studied there, so walking with him around the neighborhood on a weekday and going in and out of stores was like sliding into a buoyant, grown-up world I was not entitled to, while I'm sure that slipping into my little world was his way of reliving his years as a *lycéen,* only to thank his lucky stars for keeping them forever locked behind him. He wouldn't be surprised, he said, if I hated school. When one afternoon I showed him into my empty classroom, he was baffled to see that not a thing had changed since the days before the war. The overpowering smell of the old wooden desks still lingered in the room, he said, and that dusky slant of failing afternoon light that could smother every indecent thought in a boy's mind still swept over the dust on the dark brown furniture in my dark brown smelly classroom of Lycée J."

"Do you miss him?"

"Miss him? Not really. Maybe because,

unlike my mother, who died eight years ago, he never really died for me. He's just absent. Sometimes it's almost as though he might change his mind and slip in through a back door somewhere. Which is why I've never really mourned him. He's still around — just elsewhere." He thought for a moment.

"I've kept most of his things, his neckties especially, his rifles, golf clubs, even his old wooden tennis rackets. I used to think I was keeping them as mementos, the way I'd sealed two of his sweaters in plastic bags so that they might retain his scent. It's not death I refuse, but extinction. I'll never use his warped wooden racket, still strung with old catgut. The main reason I lament not being closer to my son now that he has children is not because I know I would have made an excellent grandfather, but because I wish he had met my father, and loved him as I did, so that now my son and I could sit together on November days like here today and remember him. There is no one to remember my father with."

"Could this be my role?" I asked completely naively.

He did not respond.

"But I should tell you that if there is one thing I regret now almost thirty years later it's that he never met you. Today this weighs on me, as if a link is missing in my life, I don't know why. Perhaps this is why I wanted to bring you here this weekend."

I was going to ask whether it wasn't perhaps too soon to meet his parents — and the thought brought a smile to my face — but I decided not to say anything, not because my ironic comment wouldn't sit well at that moment, but because a voice told me that it wasn't too soon, indeed it was about time I met or, rather, heard about his parents.

"You're scaring me a bit," I said, "because it means that I'll never pass muster unless your father approves, and since he'll never know me, you'll never approve?"

"Wrong. I know he'd approve. That's not it. I think it would have made him happy to know I've been happy this whole week." He stopped a moment. "Or is this too much pressure for those of your generation?"

I shook my head and smiled, meaning *You're so off the mark about me and my generation!*

"I've been blabbering on so much about my father that I'm sure you must think I have a father fixation. I hardly think of him. But I do dream of him. They are usually very sweet and soothing dreams. So here's a funny thing: he even knows about you. It was he who in a dream steered me away from visiting piano bars to go directly to the conservatory instead. Clearly my subconscious speaks through him."

"Would you have sought me out anyway?"

"Probably not."

"What a waste that would have been."

"Would you have come to this Sunday's concert?"

"You already asked me this."

"But you never answered."

"I know."

He nodded, meaning *My point exactly.*

After lunch he asked if I wanted to try the piano. I sat down, played a few quick chords to test it, assumed a very grave air, and then started to play "Chopsticks." He laughed. Before I knew what possessed me, I started to improvise on "Chopsticks" until I stopped and played a chaconne composed recently in the old style. I played it beautifully because I was playing it for him, because it suited autumn, because it spoke to the old house, to the boy in him still, and to the years between us I was hoping to erase.

When I stopped I asked him to tell me exactly what he had been doing when he was my age.

"Probably working in my father's law firm,

being completely miserable, because I hated it, but also because there was no one, just no one special in my life except for the . . . occasionals."

Then, from nowhere, he asked when was the last time I'd had sex.

"Promise not to laugh?"

"No."

"Last November."

"But that's a year ago."

"And even then . . ."

But I didn't finish the sentence.

"Well, the last time I brought someone to this house I was probably your age and he spent one night here and I never saw him again." He stopped short of finishing what he was about to say. He must have immediately figured what had just crossed my mind: that when he invited his lover here I wasn't born yet. Then, to change the subject, he added, "I'm sure my father would have loved the piece you played."

"Why did your father stop playing?"

"I'll never know. He played for me only once. I must have been fifteen or sixteen. He told me it was a very difficult piece. By then he had given up entirely on my musical aptitude. He sat at this very piano one day when Mother was away in Paris and there it was: a short piece played, in my opinion, magnificently, *La Chapelle de Guil-laume Tell* by Liszt. I knew right away, without a doubt, that my father was indeed a great pianist. I had seen many pictures of him in tails sitting at a piano or standing after bowing to an audience. But I had never really come face-to-face with his life as a pianist. It was a closed door. The question I'll never be able to answer is why he stopped playing, or why he never discussed it. Even when I told him once that I thought I'd heard him playing at night and that the music had drifted to my bedroom from a distant wing of the house, he denied it. 'It must have been a record,' he said. After he was done playing the Liszt that one time he simply asked, 'Did you like it?' I didn't know what to say. All I muttered was, 'I'm so proud of you.' He never expected me to say such a thing. He nodded a few times, but I could tell he was moved. Then he closed the piano, and never played for me again."

"Puzzling."

"But he wasn't a closed man at all. He liked to talk about women, especially when I was in my mid-to-late teens after one of those concerts in the church. He would speak about music but then sometimes he'd drift and end up talking about love, about the women he'd known in his younger days, and he'd speak about this intangible thing called pleasure, which no one ever really knows how to talk about, and which explains why I learned more about both pleasure and desire from him while we were walking back home from a concert than from those who were meant to help me discover what they were. He was a man who cultivated pleasure, though I doubt it was with my mother. He said so himself one day when he told me that it was far better to pay for a good half hour with a woman you might never see again than to spend time with one who leaves you more lonely after you've had a few minutes flouncing between her legs. He spoke that way. He was funny.

"One day after our Sunday concert he said that if I wanted he knew of a place where a woman could easily teach me what adults did together. I was curious and scared, but he told me where, whom to ask for, and gave me money for good measure.

"A week later we were back to our Sunday evenings together and laughing on the way. 'So it happened?' was all he asked. 'It happened,' I replied. It brought us closer still. A few weeks later I found a different kind of pleasure that he most likely knew nothing about. In retrospect, I regret never having told him about it. But in those days . . ."

He did not finish his sentence.

Did I want to go for a stroll, he asked.

I said yes.

Michel said he used to have a dog, and they would go for long walks together, returning after dark. But since the dog had died he'd never wanted another. "He suffered a lot before dying, so I put him to sleep, but I won't ever go through such a loss again."

I did not ask. But that I didn't ask must surely have warned him I'd pondered the question.

Soon we approached the wood. He said he would show me the lake. "It reminds me of Corot. It's always early evening and perpetually sunless here. Corot always has a dab of red on the boatman's bonnet in his paintings — like a sprig of mirth on gloomy November fields where there's never any snow. Reminds me of my mother — always on the verge of tears but never a sob. This landscape makes me happy, perhaps because I can feel it's gloomier than I am." When we reached the lake: "Is this where you recharge?" I asked.

"The very place!" He knew I was ribbing him.

We were going to sit on the grass, but it was damp, so we loitered by the shore a bit, then turned back.

"I don't know how to tell you this, but there is a reason why I asked you here."

"You mean it has nothing to do with my looks or my youth or the sheer brilliance of my intellect, to say nothing of my ripped body?"

He embraced me and kissed me longingly on the mouth.

"It definitely has to do with you — but I promise that what's in store will surprise you."

It was starting to get cloudy. "It really is Corot country, isn't it — mournful as ever. But it puts me in a good mood. Or maybe that's because you're here," he said.

"Clearly because I'm here." He knew I was ribbing him again. "Or maybe because I'm happy too."

"Are you really?"

"I'm trying to hide it, can't you tell?"

He put his arm around me, then kissed me on the cheek.

"Perhaps we should head back. A little Calvados wouldn't hurt."

On the way back, he said it was my turn to talk about my family. He was probably trying to show he wasn't going to do all the talking about parents and was giving me equal time to talk about mine. But there was so little to say, I said. Both my parents were amateur musicians, so I was the culmination of their dreams. My father, a university professor, was my first piano teacher but soon realized, when I was eight or so, that my capacities surpassed his. The three of us were exceptionally close. They never disagreed with me, and I could do no wrong in their eyes. I was a quiet child and by the time I was eighteen or so it was clear that my inclinations ran in all ways. I said nothing at first, but I am forever grateful that my father made it easy for us to speak about matters most parents are reluctant to even hint at. After I went to college, they separated. I think that unbeknownst to them, I was the bond that held them together, whereas they'd always had different interests, led different lives, and had very different friends. Then one day my mother ran into someone she'd known years before my father and decided to move to Milan with him. My father had altogether given up on meeting a partner but a few years later he met someone, on a train of all places, and they now have a child whose godfather and half brother I am. All told, everyone is quite happy.

"Do they know about me?" he asked.

"They do. I told him on Thursday when he called. Miranda also knows."

"Do they know I'm much older than you?"

"They do. My father, incidentally, is twice her age."

He paused a moment and was silent.

"Why did you tell them about me?"

"Because it matters, that's why. And don't ask me if it does."

We stopped walking. He scraped his shoes against a fallen branch, tore a shoot and cleaned the rest of his shoe with it, then looked at me.

"You could just be the dearest person I've ever known. Which also means you could hurt me, devastate me actually. Do people speak like this in your generation?"

"Enough with my generation! And stop saying things like this. This kind of talk upsets me."

"I won't say another word then. Do people you know ever use the big word?"

I could feel it coming. "Please hold me, just hold me."

He put his arms around me and held me tightly.

We resumed walking in silence, arm in arm, until it was my turn to scrape my shoe. "Corot country!" I cursed. It made the two of us laugh.

Back in the house: "I want to show you the kitchen. It hasn't changed in eons." We walked into a large kitchen that was clearly never meant to be a place where the owners might sit to have coffee or eggs. Pots and pans of all makes were hanging on the walls, but not in that faux, fashionably cluttered, chic French-country style found in magazines and home decor catalogues. It was ancient and dysfunctional in parts, and no one was going to hide it. As I surveyed the room I thought that it probably had electric wiring and gas and water pipes going back many decades, if not generations, that needed to be torn out and replaced.

We left the kitchen and headed to the parlor where he opened a tiny antique wooden cabinet, found a bottle, and took out two snifters, which he held in one hand with his fingers thrust between their stems. I liked how he did this.

"I'm going to show you something I believe no one has ever seen. It came into my father's hands not long after the Germans left our house. When I was in my very late twenties, and a few days before my father fell into a coma — he knew his time had come, and no one was stupid enough to try to tell him otherwise — he asked me, when we were alone together, to unlock this tiny cabinet and to take out a large leather envelope.

"My father said he was younger than I was at the time when what was in the envelope came into his possession."

"What's in it?" I asked, holding the envelope.

"Open it."

I expected some sort of deed, will, or certificate, or a compromising set of photos. Instead, when I opened the leather folio I found a musical score on eight double-sided sheets of onion paper. The staffs were drawn by the unsteady hand of someone who obviously didn't own a ruler. On the front was written: *From Léon to Adrien, January 18, 1944.*

"Adrien, my father, never explained. All he said was, 'Do not destroy it, do not give it away to some archive or library, just pass it on to someone who'll know exactly what to do with it.' It broke my heart because from the look on his face as he spoke these words I could tell he knew there was no one else in his life or in my life to give this to. I also think he knew, just knew — about me, that is. And the strange thing, as he looked at me with that deep, searching stare of those who know they are about to die, was that everything between us, every moment of love, every disappointment, every misunderstanding, every coded glance had all but dissolved. 'Find someone,' he said.

"Of course as soon as I looked at the score I was completely at a loss. Beyond the few years I'd spent playing the piano, I knew nothing about classical music, and he, on his part, never pushed me. So I never bothered with this score.

"But there was another reason why I was truly perplexed when I took a look at it. I was born twenty years after the date on the score and yet here was someone I'd never met, much less heard of, who bore my middle name, Léon. I asked my father who this man was, but he gave me a blank look, made a dismissive gesture with his hand, then said it would take too long, adding he was tired and that he preferred not to say, not to think. 'You're making me remember, and I don't want to remember,' he said. I didn't know whether it was the morphine clouding his mind or whether he was resorting to his go-to phrase — *I'd rather not say* — when trying to avoid a delicate subject, especially when he wanted you to know that if he uttered another word it would open up Pandora's box. Had I kept asking, I would have received that curt, impassive hand motion of his again, which is how he dealt with beggars he had no patience with. I'd planned to ask him again anyway, but the score slipped from my mind and I needed to care for him, as his condition kept worsening. In retrospect now, I almost think that what had kept him alive during his sickness was the need to find the chance to hand me the score without my mother's knowledge. Months after he died, I asked around and learned that not a soul on my mother's or my father's side of the family was called Léon. Finally, I asked my mother, 'Who was Léon?' She looked at me with a bewildered and amused look on her face: 'You, of course.' Had there ever been another Léon, I asked. No one. Léon had been my father's idea. They had argued about names. She wanted Michel, after my father's grandfather who had bequeathed us his property. My father insisted on Léon. She won, of course. Léon as a second name was a concession. No one ever called me that.

"Only then did it dawn on me that my mother couldn't have known anything about the existence of Léon or of the score. Had she even seen the score, she would have asked who Léon was and wouldn't have let go of the matter until she'd gotten to the bottom of it. That's the way Mother was —

intrusive and implacable once she set her mind on something. She insisted I become a lawyer — and there was no gainsaying her.

"As it turned out and after I'd made some inquiries among the staff following the death of my father, one of the older servants did recall a certain Léon. *Léon le juif,* Léon the Jew, they called him in the household, starting from my grandfather, who hated Jews, down to the cook and the chambermaids. 'But,' in the words of the same old cook, 'that was a very long time ago, before your parents even knew each other.' I could tell it was going to be like pulling teeth to get more out of our cook, so I let the matter slide, figuring I'd ask him at some other time and not give him the impression I was grilling him for answers. I asked him about the Germans who occupied our home, knowing that speaking about those days might lead us back to Léon, but all he said was that the Germans were *de vrais gentlemen* who tipped well and treated my family with exceptional respect, not like that old Jew, he said, recalling I had asked about Léon. He was the last in our family to have known Léon, but after my father died he retired and moved back to the north, where he too disappeared. So the trail went cold.

"When my mother died, I decided to sort

through the family papers — but I found nothing about the Jew. The one thing I failed to grasp was why my father had kept the score under lock and key and why I had ended up with Léon's name. What had happened to my namesake? I had hoped to find a diary or a school record of my father's early years. But my father had never kept a diary. I did find diplomas and certificates and numberless musical scores among his papers, some on paper so brittle and with such high acidic content that they crumbled as soon as you touched them. Strange to say, though, I never once saw him leaf through those scores. Occasionally, when he'd overhear pianists on the radio he would criticize their playing, always saying, 'He might as well be typing on a Remington.' Or about another world-famous pianist, 'A great pianist but an appalling musician.'

"I have no sense of how turning to law changed him or, for that matter, why he abandoned his career as a musician. Or, to put it more bluntly, I never got to know who was the man behind the man I thought my father was. I knew the lawyer only but had never even seen or met or lived with the pianist. And it kills me still today not to have known and spoken to the pianist. The person I knew was his second self. I suspect we have first selves and second selves and perhaps third, fourth, and fifth selves and many more in between."

"Whom am I speaking to now," I asked, seizing his drift, "second, third, or first self?"

"Second. I think. Age, my friend. But a part of me would die to have you speak to my younger self, to have had you here in this house when I was your age. The irony is that with you I feel your age, not mine. I am sure there'll be a price to pay for this."

"You're such a pessimist."

"Maybe. But my younger self bungled and sped through so many things. An older self is more frugal, more cautious, and therefore more reluctant — or more desperate — to rush into things he already fears he might never find again."

"But you have me here and now."

"Yes, but for how long?"

I did not answer. I was trying to avoid touching on the future, but as a result must have sounded more fatuous than he would have wished.

"This, today, like yesterday," he said, "like Thursday, like Wednesday, has been a gift. I could so easily never have found you, or never run into you again."

I didn't know what to say, so I smiled.

With that he poured each of us a second

glass of Calvados. "I hope you like this."

I nodded, as I'd done the first time with single malts.

"Fate, if it exists at all," he said, "has strange ways of teasing us with patterns that may not be patterns at all but that hint at a vestigial meaning still being worked out. My father, your father, the piano, always the piano, and then you, like my son, but not like my son, and this Jewish thread running through both our lives, all of it reminds me that our lives are nothing more than excavation digs that are always tiers deeper that we thought. Or maybe it's nothing, just nothing.

"In any case, I'll leave you with the score. I'm going to see what they're preparing for dinner tonight. Meanwhile, let me know what you think. Remember, you are one of the very, very few who have ever seen it."

He shut the door very quietly, as if to show that what I was about to do required great concentration and that the last thing he wanted was to disturb me.

I liked being alone in this room. It felt intimate, despite its large size. I even liked the smell of the old, thick curtains behind me, liked the aged mahogany paneling on the wall and the dark red rug, even liked my sunken, flaking old leather armchair, and the excellent Calvados. Everything felt aged, passed on, and set in place centuries ago for centuries to come. Wars and revolutions could not undo this because stubborn legacy and longevity seemed permanently inscribed everywhere in this mansion, down to the delicate snifter I was holding in my hand. Michel had grown up here, been sheltered here, been stifled here. I wondered if he had used this very armchair while scanning for erotic images in magazines as a teenager.

What did he expect me to do with the score — tell him it was good or bad, say the Jew was a genius? Or maybe an idiot? Or was he looking for the man his father was before becoming a father and hoping I'd help dig him out from this rubble of musical notations?

I began leafing through the score, and the more I stared at its second page the more I began to question why the staff lines were drawn in so unsteady a hand. There was only one explanation for this: there was no staved stationery available when this was written. Besides, Léon must have assumed that Adrien would immediately recognize the notes, or at least know what to do with them.

But then I began to notice something else. The score had no perceptible beginning, which meant either that the score was incomplete or that it was composed at the very peak of the modernist era. And yet, how unoriginal was that, I thought, irony bringing a smirk to my face. I looked at the last page of the score, not expecting to find a clear ending to the piece either, and indeed there was nothing but a long trill leading absolutely nowhere. How predictable, I thought, and how dull! The no-ending ending — modernism at its foulest!

Part of me didn't have the heart to tell Michel any of this. I didn't want to tell him that the score so faithfully coddled by his father and for so long was worth less than the Cartier leather folder where it had slumbered in a locked cabinet. Better to have left it sleeping.

Then as I kept leafing through the first three pages, I became aware of something that truly made my heart sink. I'd seen these notes before. Dear God, I'd even played them five years earlier in Naples! But not quite in this order. It took no time to recognize the notes. The poor fellow had been copying Mozart. How banal! And then, worse yet — I couldn't believe it — a few bars later and not so subtly, I thought I recognized wisps of something everyone knew: the recognizable lilting rondo lifted from Beethoven's *Waldstein* Sonata. Our dear Léon was stealing left and right.

I looked at the pale sepia ink. Either the ink had faded over the years or the writer was using diluted ink. It looked so desperately and hastily scribbled down, that I imagined Léon mailing it from the Gare du Nord just as the train was inching its way out to who knows where he was headed in 1944. Did its owner have a sense of humor, I thought, as he pilfered notes left and right? Was he intelligent, or a fool? Could one tell anything by the handwriting? And how old could Léon have been? A young prankster in his mid-twenties like Michel at the time, or was he even younger?

As I was trying to guess who or what Léon was, it suddenly hit me that there was a reason why I recognized the first series of notes. They were composed, or partially composed, by Mozart. But this was no sonata, no prelude, no fantasy, or fugue. This was a cadenza to Mozart's D Minor piano concerto, which was why I had recognized the theme. But he was not copying Mozart; he was quoting from Beethoven's own cadenza to Mozart's concerto, which had also inspired Léon to echo a few bars from the *Waldstein* Sonata. Léon was having fun. All he'd done was to compose the parts that the pianist Adrien was probably meant to improvise at the end of the first movement, that glorious moment when the orchestra stops and lets the pianist play at will, which is where imagination, boldness, love, freedom, prowess, talent, and a profound understanding of what lies at the very heart of Mozart's concerto can finally shout their love of music and invention in a cadenza.

The composer of the cadenza had divined what Mozart hadn't finished composing and what Mozart had left open-ended for others to finish for him, even if they composed it in an entirely different age when music had altogether changed. What one needed to enter into the mystery of Mozart's composition was not to wear Mozart's shoes or walk in his gait or echo his idiom, his voice, his pulse, his style even; what one needed was to reinvent him in ways he himself would never have imagined, to build where Mozart had stopped building, but to build what Mozart would still recognize as irreducibly his and only his.

When Michel returned I couldn't wait to tell him about the score. "This is not a sonata, it's a cadenza —" I began.

"Chicken or beef?" he interrupted. Our supper and well-being tonight trumped everything else.

I loved it when he did this. "Are we on an airplane?" I asked.

"We might serve vegan food as well," he continued, parodying an Air France stewardess. "And I have a fabulous red." He stopped a moment. "You were saying?"

"Not a sonata but a cadenza."

"A cadenza. Of course! I suspected it all along." He halted a second. "And what's a cadenza?"

I laughed.

"It's a brief one-to-two-minute moment in a piano concerto when the soloist improvises upon a theme already explored in the concerto itself. Usually, the signal for the orchestra to come clamoring back in and close the movement is a trill played by the pianist at the very end of his cadenza. I couldn't figure out what the trill was when I first saw it but now it makes perfect sense. This cadenza, however, goes on and on, I don't know for how long yet, but it's obviously more than five to six minutes long."

"So this was my father's big secret? Six minutes of music, and that's it?"

"I suppose."

"Doesn't add up, does it?"

"I'm not sure yet. I have to study this. Léon keeps echoing the *Waldstein*."

"The *Waldstein*." He repeated the word with a broad smile. It took me a moment and then, once again, I understood why he was smiling.

"Don't tell me you're twice my age and you've never heard the *Waldstein* Sonata."

"I know it inside out." Again the smile.

"You're fibbing. I know it. I can tell."

"Of course I'm fibbing."

I stood up, went to the piano, and started playing the opening bars of the *Waldstein*.

"The *Waldstein,* of course," he said.

Was he still joking?

"Actually I've heard it many times."

I stopped playing and then moved to the rondo. He said he knew it too. "Then sing it," I said.

"I'll do no such thing."

"Sing it with me," I said.

"No."

I started singing the rondo and, after a bit of coaxing by staring at him from the piano, began hearing his tentative attempts at song. I played more slowly, and then asked him to sing louder, till in the end we were singing in unison. He placed both hands on my shoulders, I thought it was a signal to stop, but then he said, "Don't stop," so I continued playing and singing. "What a voice you have," he said. "If I could, I would kiss your voice." "Keep singing," I said. So he kept singing. When I turned around at the end of our crooning, I noticed he had tears in his eyes. "Why?" I asked.

"I don't know why. Maybe because I never ever sing. Or maybe it's just this: being with you. I want to sing." "Don't you sing in the shower sometimes?" "Not in ages." I got up and, with my left thumb, wiped the tears from both his eyes. "I like that we sang," I said. "I do too," he said. "Did it make you sad?" "Not at all. I was just moved, as though you'd pushed me out of myself. I like it when you do that: push me out of myself. Plus I'm so shy that I tear up as easily as some people blush."

"You, shy? I don't think you're shy at all."

"You wouldn't believe how shy."

"You spoke to me out of nowhere, picked me up actually, and in a church of all places, and then you took me out to dinner. Shy people don't do any of this."

"The reason it happened that way is because I wasn't planning any of it, wasn't even thinking. It all came so easily, maybe because you helped. Of course I wanted to ask you to come home with me that same night, but I didn't dare."

"So you left me stranded all alone with my backpack, my bicycle, and my helmet. Thanks!"

"You didn't mind."

"I did mind. I was hurt."

"And yet now you're here with me in this room." He paused a moment. "Is this too much for you?"

"My generation again?"

We laughed.

Getting back to Léon, I took up the score.

"Let me explain to you how a cadenza works."

I riffled through his record collection — all jazz — but finally landed on a Mozart concerto. Then I located a very complex and expensive-looking music system sitting on an eighteenth-century coffee table. As I fiddled to see how it worked, I avoided looking at him so as not to give what I was about to ask any importance. "Who told you to buy this?" I asked.

"Nobody told me. I told myself. Okay?"

"Okay," I said.

He knew I liked his answer. "And I know how to work it myself. All you had to do was ask me."

It took a few moments, and we began listening to Mozart's piano concerto. I let him hear a bit of the first movement then lifted the stylus and moved it forward to the part where I suspected the cadenza started. This cadenza was composed by Mozart himself. We listened to the cadenza until I pointed out the trill that signaled the return of the full orchestra.

"That was Murray Perahia playing. Very elegant, very clear, simply superb. The key to his cadenza is these few notes taken from the main theme. I'll sing them for you and then you will too."

"Absolutely not!"

"Don't be a baby."

"No way!"

I played the notes first, then began singing as I was playing them and continued playing, to show off a bit. "Your turn now," I said while playing the notes again, and then turned my head toward him to signal it was his turn. He hesitated at first but then did as asked and began humming the notes. "You have a good voice," I finally said. Then, because I felt inspired, I played the notes once more and told him to sing them again, saying, "It would make me happy."

And he did sing again, until we sang together. "Next week I will start taking piano lessons," he said. "I want the piano to be part of my life again. Maybe I want to learn composition too."

I couldn't tell whether he was humoring me.

"Would you let me be your teacher?" I asked.

"Of course I would. What a stupid question. The question is . . ."

"Oh, shush!"

Then I told him to sit while I played Beethoven's and then Brahms's cadenzas to Mozart's D Minor concerto. "Luminous," I said, as I began playing, feeling that I was playing the two perfectly.

"There are many others. One was even composed by Mozart's own son," I said.

I played. He listened.

And then, because I felt inspired, I played him my own improvised version on the spot. "This can go on forever, if you wish."

"I so wish I could do this."

"And you will. I'd be better at the piano if I'd practiced earlier this morning, but someone had other plans for the day."

"You didn't have to agree."

"I wanted to."

Then, out of the blue: "Could you play the notes you played for your student from Thailand?"

"You mean this?" I said, knowing exactly what he was referring to.

■ ■ ■ ■

"What's interesting here is that after our friend Léon's cadenza quotes a few bars from the *Waldstein* Sonata, something far crazier happens."

"What?" he asked, almost overwhelmed by too many musical facts for one day.

I looked at the score and then once again, just to make certain that I wasn't making any of it up. "It seems to me, and I'm not sure yet, that at some point after quoting the *Waldstein* Léon dithers awhile until he slips from the Beethoven to something that very possibly inspired another piece by Beethoven, something called Kol Nidre."

"Of course," he said. He was close to laughing.

"Kol Nidre is a Jewish prayer. You see, the Jewish theme is very veiled but it's smuggled in there . . . and my hunch is that unless someone were musically trained, only a Jew who reads music would recognize that the centerpiece of this cadenza is not the Beethoven but Kol Nidre. Those few measures are repeated seven times, so Léon knew exactly what he was doing. Then, of course, he goes back to the *Waldstein,* and to the trill that announces the return of the full orchestra."

To let him know what I had in mind I played the cadenza and then Kol Nidre bit by bit for him.

"What is Kol Nidre?"

"It's an Aramaic prayer at the start of Yom Kippur, the holiest day in the Jewish calendar, and represents the recantation of all vows, all oaths, all curses, all obligations made to God. But the melody has charmed composers. My hunch is that Léon knew that your father would recognize it. It was like a coded message between them."

"But I know this tune," he suddenly said.

"Where did you hear it?"

"I don't know. I just don't know. But I know it, maybe from way, way back."

Michel thought for a moment, then, as though rousing himself, said, "I think we should sit down for dinner."

But I needed to get the matter off my chest.

"There are two ways in which your father could have known this tune. Either Léon hummed or played it for him — why, I have no idea, unless it was to prove that Jewish liturgy had beautiful music — or your father attended a Yom Kippur service, which might suggest a closer bond between the two. The service on that day is not an occasion for

tourists to come and watch how Jews celebrate the Day of Atonement."

Michel thought for a moment, then said,
"If you invited me, I'd come." I took his
hand, held it, kissed it.

During dinner we discussed what we
considered might have been the reason for
the secret cadenza. An inside joke? A distil-
lation of a work in progress? A challenge to
the pianist? Maybe a gesture from one to
the other, a salutation, in memory of a
friendship that might have lapsed, who
knows. "So many things I haven't had time
to examine yet," I said. "Unless the cadenza
was thought up in dire circumstances and
was a Jewish salvo composed from hell itself."

"Are we reading too much into this?"

"Maybe."

"We have an amazing butcher in town, so
the filet is simply excellent. And our cook
loves vegetables, asparagus if she can still
find it, which she cooks magnificently
despite her allergies. I love Indian rice, so
smell this," he said, delicately fanning the
air over the rice in my direction. He knew
he was teasing me.

But then I said there was something missing.

"Léon is Jewish, is hated by your grandparents, is most likely considered a bad influence on your father's career, and the servants think he's beneath them. France is already occupied and soon the Germans will be living under this very roof, if they aren't already eating at this very table, which you told me they did. Léon cannot be in the same house, unless he is hiding in the attic, which no one here would have tolerated. So how does the score fall into your father's hands?"

I had brought it with me to the dining table.

"Try this wine. We have three bottles left. We've let it breathe in the kitchen."

"Can you just focus, please?"

"Yes, of course. What do you think of the wine?"

"It's stunning. But why are you constantly interrupting?"

"Because I love seeing you focusing like this and I love it when you get so serious. I still can't believe you're staying with me. I can't wait to have you in my bed — can't wait."

I sipped some more wine, then he replenished my glass.

As I was cutting the meat, I couldn't help adding: "We still need to figure out how the score ended up here. Who brought it? And when? For a Jew to come here to deliver a score in 1944 seems absurd. In fact, how it got here might say everything about this score. It might even say more than the music itself."

"This makes no sense. It's like suggesting that the way a famous poem got to the printer's is more important than the poem itself!"

"In this case, it may be just so."

Michel looked at me with bewilderment, as though he had never thought of things in this twisted manner.

"Was it delivered by mail," I asked, "by hand, or did Adrien pick it up himself? Was a third party involved? A friend, or a nurse in a hospital, or someone from the camps? This is 1944 and the Germans are still occupying France. So he could have fled or been captured. If he was in the camps, which camp was it? Was he in hiding? Did he survive?"

I thought about it some more.

"There are two things that might tell us a lot. And we're missing both. Why did the composer draw the staves himself? And why are the notes so crammed together like this?"

"Why would this be important?"

"Because my hunch is that perhaps these

notes were not jotted down hastily at all." I riffled once again through the pages. "Notice, there's not a single scratch mark, nothing was crossed out where the composer might have changed his mind while composing. These notes were being transcribed, and in a place where score paper was impossible to come by, where it was even difficult to find ordinary paper. The notes are so terribly crammed — as though he were afraid he would run out of paper."

I raised the first sheet toward the candle standing in the middle of the dining table.

"What are you doing?" he asked.

"Looking for a watermark. A watermark might tell us a lot: where was the paper manufactured, in which part of France. Or elsewhere, if you follow my drift."

Michel looked at me. "I follow your drift."

Unfortunately there was no watermark on the paper. "All I can deduce is that it was cheap onion paper. So, the composer of the cadenza already knows these themes and transfers the notes in this compressed form. He wants your father to have this cadenza. This is all we know."

"No, we know something more. My father gives up playing altogether and begins to study law. The world of music is entirely shut to him. I cannot believe that this has nothing to do with Léon. Because one thing we do know. He kept this cadenza as though it were the most precious thing in his life. But then why keep it if he was never going to play it, why lock it up all those years in this cabinet — unless he promised to play it only in Léon's presence? Or unless he kept it so that someone else should materialize and play it? Someone like you, Elio!"

This flattered me but I did not want to appear to have seized what he was implying.

"Do you think he meant to return it to Léon or to someone dear to Léon? Or did he simply not know what to do with it and didn't have the heart to be rid of it — the way you continue to keep your father's tennis rackets?"

"Perhaps the most important thing is to determine who Léon was."

After dinner, using his computer I typed in Adrien's full name and within seconds saw the years when he attended the conservatory. Even his picture appeared. "Dapper and natty," I said, "and handsome." I searched for the names of teachers before, during, and after those years. The records were desultory and scattered, but in not one was there a person called Léon. I looked for Jewish-, German-, or Slavic-sounding surnames or any with *L* as a first initial. Nothing there either. I looked for students with the name Léon. Nothing. Either he had another name or his name was removed from the school records. Or he'd never been at the conservatory. "There is no Léon," I finally said.

"So here ends our bit of detective work."

By then, we were sitting very close together on the sofa, the light was dim, and we were drinking more Calvados.

"Perhaps your father studied with Alfred Cortot. But I doubt that Léon did."

"Why, do you think?"

"Cortot was anti-Semitic and became even more so under the occupation. I believe the violinist Thibaud, whom Cortot knew well, played for the Führer."

"Terrible times."

"Any more thoughts on the matter?" he asked.

"Why do you ask?"

He shook his head ever so mildly. "No reason. I just love being like this with you. Talking the way we do, at night, in this room, sitting on this sofa, glued together while you're fiddling with the computer, and outside all over, it's just November. I love that you've taken such an interest."

"I love it too, very much."

"And yet you don't believe in fate."

"I told you, I don't think in those terms."

"Then maybe when you get to be my age and the dearth of things life has to offer becomes more evident by the day, maybe then you can start noticing those tiny accidents that turn out to be miracles and that can redefine our lives and cast an incandescent luster over things that, in the great scheme of things, could easily be meaningless. But this is not meaningless."

"This here tonight is wonderful."

"Yes, it is wonderful." But he said it with a tone of nostalgic resignation verging on melancholy, as though I were a dish he was watching being taken away before he'd had his fill. Is this what happens when one is close to twice someone's age: one starts losing people long before they've started looking elsewhere?

We sat this way without saying anything. I gave him what I thought was a hug, but what he returned was a real, sad, famished hug filled with sensual despair.

"What's wrong?" I asked, still reluctant to hear what I already suspected was going to be his answer.

"Not a thing. But then this is what's so scary — if you see my drift — precisely because there's nothing wrong."

"Give me more Calvados."

He was happy to oblige. He stood up, walked over to the small cabinet behind one of the speakers, and took out another bottle. "Much better quality."

He knew I had changed the subject. I was hoping that something would lift this sudden cloud between us, but nothing came, and neither he nor I attempted to dispel it, perhaps because neither was quite sure what lurked behind it. So he enlightened me about the Calvados, and its history, and I listened, and read the tiny hand scrawl on the bottle's label giving a history of the house that produced it. Which was when he had a stroke of genius, and used an expression that had become a catchphrase between the two of us: "I want to make you happy." I knew exactly what he meant. "So, keep reading the label, I don't want you distracted. I don't even want you looking."

He picked up the glass of Calvados and sipped from it. Then I felt it, felt his mouth, felt the slight tingling. "I love what you're doing," I finally said, shutting my eyes, trying to put the bottle down somewhere until I decided to place it on the carpet, at the foot of the sofa.

I remembered the housemaid.

"Gone already. Didn't you hear her car?"

■ ■ ■ ■

We spent Sunday in the house. As Michel remembered, it always seemed to rain on Sundays, and the wood, where we'd planned to take a long walk, was growing darker and bleaker by the hour. Late that morning I practiced for a couple of hours while he leafed through some papers from his office. But ours was mostly perfunctory activity, and in the end we were both relieved when the other tactfully suggested that perhaps it might be good to head back to Paris before traffic got heavy with Parisians returning late from the weekend. As we neared the city, there was a slightly awkward moment when it became clear he was planning to drop me at my address first — and that he was doing so either because he didn't want me to feel pressured to head straight to his home or because he suspected I had other plans before our evening concert. Or, I thought, he needed some time alone. After all, he had a habit of coming back to Paris on Sundays, and who knows, perhaps this was what he'd done for years and didn't want it changed. When he double-parked in front of the entrance to my building, he didn't turn off the engine. I was meant to step out, which I did. "See you in a bit," I said, to which he gave that silent, wistful nod of his. And then I simply found the courage. "I don't need to go home. I don't want to go home." "Get back in," he said. "I adore you, Elio, I adore you." We went straight to his home. We made love, even dozed a bit, then quickly rushed to the concert, followed by the intermission cider, and then the three-course meal during which he held my hand. "Tomorrow is Monday," he said. "Last week's Monday was agony." Why, I asked. But I knew the answer. "Because I felt I'd lost you — and for what reason? Because I was scared you'd say no and was trying not to seem depraved."

He looked at me for a while. "Do you have to go home tonight?"

"Do you want me to?"

"We'll pretend we met tonight and that instead of walking away with your bike, you said, 'I want to sleep with you, Michel.' Would you have said it?"

"I was on the verge of saying it. But no! You, sir, had to walk away!"

Monday morning I decided to take a taxi and went straight home to change. The place looked slightly unfamiliar, as though I hadn't been there for weeks, months. The last time I'd seen morning there was on Saturday when I'd dashed upstairs, picked up a few things to wear, and rushed down to where he was waiting in his car. That afternoon, after teaching, I headed straight to the conservatory office to find whatever I could about Léon.

When I saw Michel at our usual bistro that night I told him that the trail had gone cold. Not a trace of Léon anywhere. He was more disappointed than I'd expected, which was why I had another idea on Tuesday. I tried two music schools and searched their yearly records. But once again, nothing.

We both made the reasonable assumption that either Léon had studied abroad or that, like well-off Jews in the early years of the century, he had studied with a private tutor. Two more days went by this way. I had run out of clues.

On Friday, however, I finally discovered Léon's identity in the records of the lycée where both Michel and his father had been enrolled and where the secretary had searched through the records in my pres-ence after I'd claimed to be Michel's nephew. In the car to the country that day, I couldn't hold back and broke the news to him. "I was even able to obtain his old address. The family name is Deschamps. The only problem is that Deschamps is not exactly a Jewish name."

"Could be an acquired or changed name. Think of Feldmann, Feldenstein, Feldenblum, or just Feld."

"Could be. But there are many Léon Deschampses on the Web, assuming they are all alive, or still live in France. The search could take months."

He looked perplexed. What I couldn't help thinking was why he hadn't made the school connection himself. Finally, I asked him why after all those years he was still searching for Léon.

"It may tell me something about my father that I never knew. I'm also curious to know when and how Léon disappeared."

"But why?"

"I don't know why. Maybe it's just a way of reaching my father, to know what made him stop doing what he loved most, and to understand his friendship or love for Léon, if love and friendship it was. It's the one thing my father never mentioned and yet by the time I was eighteen he could easily have opened up to me. Or perhaps I was not unlike my own son and was trying to put some distance between us. Or maybe it's my way of atoning for not making time to know the

266

man who'd stopped playing music. But how many of us ever make time to know who our parents really were? How many sunken layers deep are those we thought we knew simply because we loved them?"

"In any event," I said, interrupting him, "I've even found Léon's picture in the yearly class photo. Here, take a look." I produced the photo I'd had copied that same day in the school office. "He is very handsome. And looks very Catholic, very conservative."

"Indeed. Very handsome," said Michel.

"Are you thinking what I'm thinking?" I asked.

"Of course I'm thinking what you're thinking. It's what we've been thinking all along, isn't it?"

When we arrived, the first thing he did after depositing his bag and greeting the cook was to head directly to the living room, open a slim drawer in a little table by the French windows, and produce a large envelope. "Take a look," he said.

It was a blown-up old class photograph, taken a year or two before the one I'd had reproduced. He pointed at Adrien with his pinkie; he looked younger in this picture. We were both looking for Léon.

"Find him?" he asked. I shook my head.

267

But then there he was, standing right next to Adrien. The resemblance between the face in my photograph and in the old class photograph was stunning. "So you knew all along!" I said.

He nodded with a guiltily amused smile. "I knew about the picture. But I needed someone else to confirm it."

I thought about this for a while.

"Is that why you brought me here last week?"

"I knew you were going to ask this. The answer is no. There was another reason, and I'm sure you've guessed it. I want to give you the score. By giving it to you, and to no one else, I am fulfilling my father's last wish. All I ask is that you play it at a concert."

A heavy silence fell between us. I wanted to protest and say what people say when they're given an expensive gift: *I can't accept it* — which also means *I am not worthy of your gift.* But I knew this would offend him.

"I still think our discovery is too neat, too easy," I said. "Part of me doesn't trust it. Let's not rush to conclusions yet."

"Why not?"

"Because I can't think of a single reason why a well-to-do young Catholic man from the Lycée J. whose parents probably subscribed to the *Action Française* would want

268

to touch Kol Nidre."

"So what are you saying?"

"That our Léon may not be Léon Deschamps."

In my attempt not to leave any stones un-turned, I spent the whole of the following week looking for clues.

There were more dead ends, and another false start, but then, that Saturday afternoon in his country house, it suddenly hit me.

"Something kept gnawing at me. First that your father continued to go to the Sainte U. concerts on Sundays. Might the church have been tied in some mysterious way to Léon? Perhaps the church itself also had something to do with the Florian Quartet. I knew that the Florian had been playing for years at that same church and you yourself told me that your father had subsidized their concerts. So I looked them up online and eventually found out, as I suspected, that there were not one or two, but three incar-nations of the Florian. The Florian started in the mid-1920s, not as a quartet but as a trio: violin, cello, and piano. And now comes the part that shows I'm a true genius. The pianist of the trio was not Léon Deschamps, as the two of us thought, but someone who had been with the trio for ten years, who played the piano but also the violin. His name was Ariel Waldstein. So I looked up Ariel Waldstein and sure enough he was a Jewish pianist who didn't just die in the camps but was beaten to death there because he owned an Amati violin and refused to part with it. He was sixty-two years old."

"But the name Ariel is not Léon," said Michel.

"I put the puzzle together early this morning — how, I've no idea. In Hebrew Ariel means 'lion of God': in short, Léon. Many Jews have a Jewish and a Latin name. In the twenties the violinist is listed as Ariel; in the early thirties he becomes Léon, probably because of rising anti-Semitism. The easiest way to find out more about him is to inquire at Yad Vashem in Jerusalem."

I felt I needed to add something else here, as though all this digging and excavating into the life of Ariel Waldstein were also bringing to light a subject that might seem totally incidental but that I knew was subliminally related if only because it involved the passage of time and the rediscovery of a beloved person. I could almost sense where this could head and was already reluctant to fathom any deeper for fear that Michel's thoughts were already inclined that way. He didn't bring it up, I didn't either.

But I was sure it had crossed his mind.

We showered together that Sunday morning, then went out for a short walk, using the back door, which I hadn't seen before. Everyone in the village seemed to know Monsieur Michel and greetings flew back and forth across the way. He led me to a café on the corner of a street that looked as though it had nothing to recommend it, but the moment we stepped inside, I immediately felt warm and sheltered. It was filled with people who had parked their cars or vans to have something hot to drink before getting back on the road. We ordered two cups of coffee and two croissants. Three girls in their late twenties were sitting next to us, basically grumbling about the men in their lives. I liked it when Michel, who was eavesdropping, smiled and then winked at me. "Men are terrible," he said to one of the girls. "Horrible. How you men can face yourselves every morning is beyond me." "It's not easy, but we try," said Michel. There was laughter. The waiter, who overheard, said that women were better than men and that his wife was the most perfect person in the world. "Why?" asked one of the girls who kept going through the motions of lighting a cigarette only to put off doing so. "Why? Because she made me a better person. And let me tell you, with me this was something only a saint could accomplish." "So she is a saint then." "Let's not exaggerate. Who wants a saint in bed." Everyone was laughing.

After coffee Michel extended his legs all the way under the table and seemed majestically satisfied with breakfast. "Another?" he asked. I nodded yes. Michel ordered two more coffees. We didn't speak. "Three weeks," he finally said, perhaps to fill the silence. I echoed his words. Then, from nowhere, he reached out and held my hand. I left it in his, feeling awkward because the place was filled with people who were standing at the bar. He must have sensed my unease, and let go. "Tonight they're playing Beethoven again." He was saying it as though tacitly trying to coax me into going.

"I thought we had a date."

"Well, I didn't want to presume," he said.

"Stop!"

"I can't help it."

"But why?"

"Because the young teenager still lingers inside me, and occasionally utters a few words, then ducks and goes into hiding. Because he's afraid of asking, because he thinks you'll laugh that he asked, because

272

even trusting is difficult. I'm shy, I'm scared, and I'm old."

"Don't think this way. We've almost solved a mystery today. What we need to do is ask the cellist tonight if he remembers Ariel. He may not, but all the same, we'll ask."

"Will it bring my father back?"

"No, but it might make him happy, which will make you happy."

He considered my words for a moment, then shook his head as he'd done before, to signify resigned and quiet comprehension. Then, as though he'd jumped across all the unstated subjects between us: "Can you promise that you'll play the cadenza — one day soon, I hope?"

"I'll play it late this coming spring when I tour the States, and in the fall when I'm back in Paris. I promise."

I saw him hesitate and I realized why. Now was the time to tell him.

"In America, I'm planning to drop in on someone I haven't seen in ages."

I watched him ponder the matter.

"So you're traveling solo then?"

I nodded.

Again I watched him weigh my words.

"The marriage canard?" he finally asked.

I nodded. I loved that he was able to read me so well, yet I feared what he was reading. "Being with you reminds me of him," I said. "If I meet him, the first thing I'll want to do is tell him about you."

"What, that I fall short of such a high standard?"

"No, because you and he are the standard. Now that I think of it, there's only been the two of you. All the others were occasionals. You have given me days that justify the years I've been without him."

I looked at him, and this time it was I who reached out and held his hand.

"Walk?" I said.

"Walk."

We stood up and he suggested we go back through the wood to reach the lake.

"What I think we should do is find out who Ariel Waldstein was. Perhaps there is someone who might know more about him."

"Perhaps. But he was sixty-two when he died, which puts a living relative at a very, very advanced age."

"So Ariel was probably twice your father's age at the time."

He suddenly looked at me and smiled.

"You're a snake!"

"I wonder about the two of them. Maybe this is what feeds our search in the end."

"Us, you mean?"

"Maybe. If the church has records, we'll

know. We can even try to find Ariel's address, maybe in an old telephone book. And if we do find the building, what we should do is commission a *Stolperstein* in his name."

"But what if there are no descendants, what if the line stopped with him, what if there isn't a trace of him and there is not a thing more to learn?"

"Then we'll have done a good deed. The stone will be in memory of all those who perished and couldn't even smuggle a word of warning or of love or even their name before the gas chamber. Except for a score with a Hebrew prayer. Did anyone in your family die in the Shoah?"

"You know about my great-uncles. I also think my great-grandmother died in Auschwitz. But I'm not sure. You die and then no one speaks of you, and before you know it, no one asks, no one tells, no one even knows or wants to know. You're extinct, you never lived, never loved. Time never casts shadows and memory doesn't drop ashes."

I thought of Ariel. The score was his love letter to a young pianist, his secret missive. *Play it for me. Say Kaddish for me. Remember the tune? It's hidden in there, under the Beethoven, next to the Mozart, find me.* Who knows under what dreadful, unthinkable conditions Léon the Jew penned his cadenza to say, *I am thinking of you. I love you, play.*

And I thought of old Ariel the Jew who'd visit Adrien's home even though he knew he was unwelcome, Ariel seeking refuge but being turned out or, worse yet, denounced either by the father or by the mother or by the servants, probably with the blessing of the parents. I thought of Ariel attempting to flee to Portugal, or England, or far worse, Ariel arrested by the French Milice during one of those terrifying raids when Jews young and old were torn from their homes in the middle of the night and forced into packed trucks. Then Ariel penned up somewhere, Ariel in the cattle cars, and finally Ariel being beaten to death because he wouldn't part with his violin, which is likely now sitting in a German home with a family who might not even know the instrument was looted after its owner perished in a camp. Was Michel's father perhaps atoning for not having helped to save Ariel? *Since I couldn't give you and your loved ones shelter, I'll never play again.* Or: *After what they've done to you, music is dead to me.* I could just hear the older man imploring: *But you must play. For the love of me, never stop, play this then.*

And once again I thought of my life. Was

there anyone who would send me a cadenza one day and say, *I am gone, but please find me, play for me?*

"What is the name of the Jewish prayer?"

"Kol Nidre."

"Is it recited for the dead?"

"No, that prayer is called the Kaddish."

"Do you know it?"

"Every Jewish boy learns it. We're taught to rehearse for the death of loved ones before we know what death even is. The irony is that the Kaddish is the only prayer one cannot use on oneself."

"Why is that?"

"Because you can't recite it and be dead at the same time."

"You people!"

We laughed. Then I thought for a moment. "You know, there is more than a strong possibility that this whole Léon-Ariel thing is nothing more than fiction."

"Yes, but it is ours. I know exactly what we'll do tonight. We'll return to the city, I will be like my father, and you'll be the young man I was in those years, or you'll be my son whom I never see, and we'll sit together and listen to the Florian Quartet, perhaps the way my father did, when he was your age and I was Léon's. You know, life is not so original after all. It has uncanny ways

277

of reminding us that, even without a God, there is a flash of retrospective brilliance in the way fate plays its cards. It doesn't deal us fifty-two cards; it deals, say, four or five, and they happen to be the same ones our parents and grandparents and great-grandparents played. The cards look pretty frayed and bent. The choice of sequences is limited: at some point the cards will repeat themselves, seldom in the same order, but always in a pattern that seems uncannily familiar. Sometimes the last card is not even played by the one whose life ended. Fate doesn't always respect what we believe is the end of a life. It will deal your last card to those who come after. Which is why I think all lives are condemned to remain unfinished. This is the deplorable truth we all live with. We reach the end and are by no means done with life, not by a long stretch! There are projects we barely started, matters unresolved and left hanging everywhere. Living means dying with regrets stuck in your craw. As the French poet says, *Le temps d'apprendre à vivre il est déjà trop tard,* by the time we learn to live, it's already too late. And yet there must be some small joy in finding that we are each put in a position to complete the lives of others, to close the ledger they left open and play their last card for them. What could be more gratifying than to know that it will always be up to someone else to complete and round off our life? Someone whom we loved and who loves us enough. In my case, I'd like to think it will be you, even if we're no longer together. It's like already knowing who will be the one who'll shut my eyes. I want it to be you, Elio."

For a moment, and just as I was listening to Michel speak, it occurred to me that there was only one person on this planet that I'd like to have my eyes shut by. And he, I hoped, without saying a word to me for years, would cross the globe to place his palm upon my eyes, as I would place mine on his.

"So," said Michel, "we'll meet the oldest member of the quartet, the one you were keen on hearing three weeks ago, and we'll ask if he remembers. But before that, during the break, we'll buy hot cider from the decrepit old nun, maybe pretend again that we don't know each other, promise to meet after the concert, knowing that afterward we'll head out for a little snack."

"God, I did tell you how much I wanted you to hold me and ask me to come home with you that night? I was almost on the point of saying something but then I held back."

"Perhaps it wasn't in the cards that night." He smiled.

"Perhaps not."

He looked at me while wrapping his scarf around his neck. "Are you cold?" he asked.

"A bit," I said. I could tell he was feeling apprehensive about me but didn't want to show it. "Want to go back home instead?"

I shook my head. "I get cold when I'm nervous."

"Why are you nervous?"

"I don't want this to end."

"Why should it?"

"No reason."

"You are the one card I was almost cheated of in this lifetime. Tonight it will be three weeks, and it could so easily not have happened at all. I need —" But then he stopped.

"You need?"

"I need another week, another month, another season, meaning another lifetime. Give me winter. Come spring, you'll fly away on tour. Beneath all the layers we uncovered today, I know there is one person for you, and I don't believe it's me."

I did not say anything. He smiled wistfully.

"The marriage canard perhaps." Then he balked for a moment, and I heard his voice tighten. "The one thing I want in this life is for you to find happiness. The rest . . ." He couldn't finish his sentence. He shook his head to mean that the rest didn't matter.

Neither of us had anything to add. I held him and he held me, and we were still holding each other when he spotted a skein of geese flying overhead. "Look!" he said. I did not release my hold.

"November," I said.

"Yes. Not winter, not fall. I've always liked November in Corot country."

■ ■ ■ ■

CAPRICCIO

■ ■ ■ ■

Erica and Paul.

They had never met before, yet both stepped out of the same elevator together. She was wearing high heels, he boat shoes. Riding to my floor, they'd discovered they were headed to the same apartment and that they even knew someone in common, a certain Clive about whom I knew nothing whatsoever. How they managed to arrive at Clive struck me as strange, but then why find anything strange on an evening that already promised to be strange, since the two persons I so desperately wanted to see at my farewell party had in fact arrived together. He came with his significantly older boyfriend, she with her husband, but I still couldn't believe that, after months of wanting to draw closer to the two of them, I finally had them both under my roof on my last few days in the city. There were many others present — but who cared about the other guests: his partner, her husband, the yoga instructor, the friend Micol kept saying I had to meet, the couple I befriended last fall at a conference on Jewish expatriates from the Third Reich, the peculiar acupuncturist from 10H, the crazy logician from my department along with his nutty vegan wife, and sweet Dr. Chaudhuri from Mount Sinai who'd been happy to reinvent the very concept of finger food tonight to accommodate the guests. At some point we uncorked the prosecco and everyone drank to our return to New Hampshire. The speeches echoed in the already empty apartment and a few graduate students toasted and roasted me with affection and humor, as more guests kept coming and going.

But the two who mattered stayed. There was even a moment, as people were milling around the barren apartment, when she stepped out onto the balcony and I followed, then he followed, and the two of them leaned against the banister with flutes in hand, talking about this man Clive, she at my left, he at my right, while I set my glass down on the floor and put my arms around each of their waists, friendly, casual, totally okay. Then I removed my arms and leaned against the balustrade, all three of us shoulder to shoulder, watching the setting sun together.

Neither shifted away from me. Both were leaning into me. It had taken months to bring them here. This was our quiet moment on the balcony overlooking the Hudson on this unusually warm mid-November evening.

His department at the university was on the same floor as mine, but we had no academic dealings with each other. From the looks of him, I assumed he was either a graduate student finishing his dissertation or a recent postdoc or an early-tenure-track assistant professor. We shared the same stairway and the same floor, occasionally crossed paths at large faculty meetings, or more commonly at Starbucks two blocks down Broadway, usually late in the afternoon before graduate seminars started. We'd also noticed each other when we met a few times in the same salad bar across the street and then couldn't avoid smiling when we ran into each other after lunch to brush our teeth in the same bathroom. It became a standing source of smiles when the two of us met on our way to the men's room with our toothpaste already spread on our brushes. Neither, it seemed, brought his tube to the bathroom. One day he looked at me and asked, "Aquafresh?" and I said yes.

How did he know? By the stripes, he replied. And so to seize his opening, I asked which brand he used. "Tom's of Maine." I should have known. He was definitely a Tom's of Maine type. Probably used Tom's deodorant, Tom's soap, and other non-mainstream products found mostly in health food stores. Sometimes, after watching him rinse out the toothpaste, I wanted to know how fennel after salad tasted in his mouth.

We weren't courting each other but an implicit something seemed to hover between us. Our frail pontoon bridge was built over shy afternoon pleasantries and then hastily dismantled the next morning with scarcely a greeting when we happened to take the same stairway. I wanted something, and I suspect he did too. But I was never sure I'd read the situation clearly enough to say anything or move things farther along. During one of our brief exchanges, I took the opportunity to tell him that I was coming to the end of my sabbatical and would soon be moving back to New Hampshire. He said he was sorry to hear this; he'd meant to sit in on my seminar about the Pre-Socratics. "But time!" he said. "Time!" mingling an awkward, apologetic smile with a modest sigh. So he'd looked me up and knew about my seminar on the Pre-Socratics. This was flattering. He was on deadline for his book on the Russian pianist Samuil Feinberg. I had never heard of Feinberg before and felt it added another side to him I wished I'd taken the time to know better. If he was free and wanted to come for a small farewell reception in our nearly empty apartment — there were no more than four chairs left, I said — he'd be more than welcome. Would he? Definitely, he said. His reply came so quickly I was tempted not to believe him.

Then there was Erica. We were in the same yoga class, sometimes she was there unusually early — six a.m. — as was I; sometimes the two of us showed up very late, at six p.m. There were even times when we came twice on the same day, at six a.m. and at six p.m., almost as though we'd been looking for each other but knew better than to hope to meet twice on the same day. She liked her corner, and I was always a foot away. Even when she wasn't there, I liked to lay my mat on the floor about four feet out from the wall. At first it was because I liked our usual spot, later I found subtle ways of saving her spot for her. But neither of us was a regular, which was why it took ages to exchange so much as a hasty nod. Sometimes when I was already lying down with my eyes shut, I would suddenly hear someone drop a mat next to mine. Without looking, I knew who it was. Even when she approached our narrow corner on bare feet, I'd learned to recognize her stealthy, timid swish, the sound of her breathing, the way she cleared her throat once she'd lain down. She made no secret of acting surprised yet pleased to see me there. I was more circumspect and would pretend to do a double take with a sudden *Oh, it's you* look. I didn't want to be obvious, nor give the impression that I was either eager to connect beyond what had always been light, perfunctory yoga chitchat whenever we gathered outside the studio with our shoes off waiting for the earlier group to vacate the room. There was something always civil yet mildly ironic when we discussed our mediocre performance in class, or complained about the bad substitute teacher, or sighed, wishing each other a pleasant weekend after hearing a stormy weather forecast. We both knew that none of this was going anywhere. But I liked her slim feet, and her smooth shoulders gleaming with a summer's tan that seemed to resent letting the scent of last weekend's sunscreen wear off. Above all I liked her forehead, which was not flat but rounded and which hinted at thoughts I couldn't put into words but wanted to know better, because there was a wry afterthought visibly floating on her features every time she flashed a smile. She wore tight clothes with her lean calves exposed so that, if I allowed my mind free rein, I could easily imagine her legs raised ninety degrees in a *viparita karani* pose with her heels resting against my chest, toes reaching my shoulders, ankles cupped in my hands as I knelt facing her. Then if she'd bend her legs and gradually tuck her knees around my waist, all I would need was to hear her breathe and utter a moan to know that what I wanted was more than just yoga fellowship.

I was thinking of inviting our yoga teacher for a farewell evening, I said. Would she and her husband like to join us? That would be great, she said.

So here they both were. It was warm for November, and our French windows were wide open, and a breeze from the river kept wafting across the room, while candles flickered on the windowsills, and all of us felt we were in a movie spending the most enchanted Saturday evening where not a thing goes wrong. All I did was introduce people to people and pose questions, deftly, so nothing I asked might sound like those hackneyed, typically rehearsed host questions if I sensed that a conversation was drying up. *What did you make of the final scene in the movie? What did you think of those two aging actors? Did you like the movie as much as the director's previous one? I find myself liking movies that suddenly end with a song. Do you?*

It was my farewell party but I was still the evening's host. I made sure the prosecco kept flowing freely, and everyone seemed completely relaxed. You could see it in the way the two were leaning against the wall and chatting, and, when I'd occasionally join them, I felt we were a band apart. If everyone had left the room, we wouldn't have noticed and would have gone on talking about this or that book, this movie or that play, every subject flowing into the other with never a disagreement.

They asked questions too — of me, of each other, and once or twice would turn to those who'd approached us by the kitchen to draw them into the conversation. We burst out laughing and I held their hands, and I know they both liked that I'd done it and they responded with a gentle squeeze of their own that was neither lax nor merely politely reciprocal. At some point he, and later she, rubbed my back, delicately, almost as if they also liked the feel of my sweater and wanted to feel it again. It was an amazing evening, we were drinking, our cell phones had not rung once, and Dr. Chaudhuri's dessert would start coming out soon. The party had been supposed to end at eight thirty but it was well past that and no one gave a sign of wanting to leave.

Occasionally I would sneak a glance at Micol meaning *Things okay at your end?* to which a hasty nod would mean *Yes — all okay at yours? Good enough here,* I'd respond. We were a perfect team, and being a team is what had kept us together. It was why, I think, we'd always known we'd make a good couple. Teamwork, yes. And sometimes passion.

What's with these two? she signaled with an inquiring tilt of her head, meaning the two young guests she'd never seen before. *Tell you later,* I signaled back. She looked pinched and a bit suspicious. I knew that killjoy look that said, *You're up to something.*

The two had a sense of humor and laughed quite a bit, sometimes at my expense since I was seldom up-to-date with things everyone else seemed to know. But I let them have their fun.

At some point Erica interrupted and whispered: "Don't look now, but your wife's friend keeps staring at us."

"She's interested in a job at the university,

which is why I've been avoiding her."

"Not interested?" he asked, a smidgen of irony in his voice.

"Or not convinced?" she threw in.

"Not impressed," I replied. "What I meant to say was *not attracted.*"

"She's pretty, though," Erica said. I shook my head with a derisive smile.

"Quiet! She knows we're talking about her."

All three of us looked sheepishly away. "Plus her name is Kirin," I added.

"Not Kirin, it's Karen," he said.

"I heard Kirin."

"Actually, she did say Kirin," said my yoga partner.

"That's because she speaks Michigander."

"You mean Michiganese."

"Sounds meshuga." We burst out laughing. We couldn't seem to control ourselves.

"We're being watched," he said.

As we were still trying to muffle our laughter, my mind raced ahead of me. I wanted them in my life. And under any conditions. I wanted them now, with his boyfriend, her spouse, whatever, with their newborns or adopted children if they had them. They'd be welcome to come and go as they pleased, just be in my humdrum, ever-so-boring day-to-day life in New

Hampshire.

And what if Erica and Paul got to like each other in some other, unforeseen manner — which might not be so unforeseen at all?

It might even give me a vicarious thrill. The libido accepts all currencies, and vicarious pleasures have an over-the-counter exchange rate that is considered reliable enough to pass for real. No one ever went bankrupt borrowing someone else's pleasure. We go bankrupt only when we want no one. "Do you think she could make anyone happy?" I asked about my wife's friend, not knowing why exactly I had asked the question. "A man like you?" he immediately added as though ready to aim a quick dart, while her sly but tacit smile, following his, told me she might have read the ulterior meaning of my question. Both seemed to agree that I was not the type who was easily made happy. "If you only knew how simple are the things I want." "Like?" she asked, almost too abruptly, as though eager to catch me waffling or fibbing. "I can name two." "Name them, then," she said, challenging me on the spot without realizing that she had spoken too hastily and that my answer, clearly hanging on the tip of my tongue, wasn't what she expected at all.

Noticing I hesitated, he said, "Maybe he doesn't want to answer." "Perhaps I do," I replied. Again a rueful smile quivered on her lips. "Perhaps not." *So now she knows, she must know.* I could tell I was making her nervous. But this, I knew from experience, was the moment when the bold question is asked, or doesn't even need to be asked, because the answer can only be yes. But she was nervous. "Most of our wants are imaginary anyway, aren't they?" I said, trying once more to soften what I'd just said to give her an out in case she was looking for one and couldn't find it. "And some of our fondest desires end up meaning more to us unrealized than tested — don't you think?"

"I don't think I've ever waited long enough to know what delayed desires are." He burst out laughing.

"I have," she said.

I looked at them, and they looked at me. I liked awkward moments like these. Sometimes all I needed was to draw them out and not rush to nip them in the bud. But the tension was rising and she hastened to say something, anything, which also told me she had indeed intuited what I wasn't saying: "I'm sure there must have been someone who bruised you once, or scarred you."

"There was," I replied. "Some people leave us scuttled and damaged." I thought awhile. "In my case I'm the one who did the scuttling, yet I'm the one who never recovered."

"Has she?"

I hesitated a moment. "He," I corrected.

"Where?"

"Italy."

"Italy, of course. They do things differently there."

She is clever, I thought.

Erica and Paul.

So, yes, they did get along. I let them talk and walked over to some of the other guests. I even joked a bit with Micol's friend who, despite the birthmark, was not without beauty and a lively sense of irony, which told me she was a gifted and talented aspiring critic.

For a fleeting moment, my mind traveled back to all the weekends during the last academic year when friends from the university would come for our usual informal Sunday dinner. We'd have our traditional chicken potpie, the quiches — both bought and ready to be warmed — plus my signature cabbage salad with all kinds of ingredients thrown in. Someone always brought cheeses, and someone else, dessert. And there'd be lots of wine and good bread. We'd talk about Greek triremes and Greek fire and about Homeric similes and Greek rhetorical figures in modern authors. I'll be losing all this, the way I'd lose my small New York rituals, acquired without my knowledge, and that I'd learn to miss when I was elsewhere. I'd lose my colleagues and my new friends, to say nothing of the two of them as well, especially now that we'd learned to be informed with each other outside of yoga and the academy.

I looked around now and saw that the place was as empty as when Micol and I moved in last August. A table, four chairs, a few weather-beaten deck chairs, a sideboard, empty bookcases, one sunken sofa, a bed, closets with countless hangers dangling like stuffed birds with their wings stretched out, and that desolate grand piano that neither Micol nor I had ever even touched and that was still piled with the playbills we kept promising to take back to New Hampshire but already knew we never would. Everything else was already packed and shipped. The university had extended our stay until mid-November, which was when the next tenant, also in the Classics Department, was due to arrive. Maynard and I had been in graduate school together and I'd already written him a welcoming note. *The dryer takes too long and the Wi-Fi is unreliable.* I'd never envied him. Now I'd trade his lot for mine in a second.

Eventually, and just as I'd predicted, the two started talking about Clive the journalist again, whose last name neither of them remembered. Paul was wearing a bleached-white short-sleeve linen shirt with the chest button wide open. When he raised his elbow and brought his hand to his head to recall Clive's surname, I could see the skin of his arm all the way up to the scantiest tuft of hair under his arm. He probably shaves there, I thought. I loved his glistening wrists — so thoroughly tanned. I could just see myself spending the rest of the evening trying to catch him raising his hand to his head the next time he'd try to remember someone's name.

On occasion, I'd catch him exchanging an elusive and hasty glance with his boyfriend across the room. Collusion and solidarity — something sweet in the way they seemed to look out for each other.

She had come wearing a loose sky-blue

blouse. I couldn't quite stare at her chest because its contour was just subtle enough not to be provocative, but I knew she was aware each time I looked. I'd never seen her except in yoga clothes. It was her dark eyebrows and large, hazel eyes that drew me — they didn't just stare at you, they asked something of you and then lingered as though actually expecting an answer, to which your speechless, blank stare spelled a failure to respond. But they weren't quite asking anything either — they had the look of total familiarity of someone who remembers you, and is trying to place where from, and the suggestion of a jeer in her eyes was just her way of saying you weren't helping her remember because she could tell you remembered but were pretending not to. There was, and I'd been noticing it too often, something implied each time her eyes strayed to me; it had almost made me break the silence between us once when I saw her waiting in line at a movie theater. She was with her husband, saying something to him, when suddenly she turned and looked at me, and for a brief moment neither of us stopped staring until we both recognized each other, did some silent backpedaling, and simply flashed a silent nod hello, meaning *Yoga, right? Yes, yoga.* Then we let our gazes scamper away.

Meanwhile, Micol and the yoga teacher decided to step out onto the balcony to light cigarettes. He was making her laugh. I liked hearing her laugh; she seldom laughs — we seldom laugh. I bummed a cigarette from one of the other guests and joined them. "We've packed away all our ashtrays," my wife explained, holding a half-emptied plastic glass on the rim of which she tapped the ashes of her cigarette. "No willpower," said the yoga instructor about himself. "None here either," she responded, both of them laughing now as he reached for her cup and tapped his ashes. We chitchatted a while longer until something totally unexpected happened.

Someone had opened the piano and was already playing what I instantly recognized as a piece attributed to Bach. When I stepped back into the room, the crowd had huddled around the piano to listen to what I should have guessed but didn't want to guess was Paul playing. For a moment, and perhaps because I wasn't expecting it, I was transfixed on the spot. We had already shipped the rugs back and the sound was far clearer, richer, and it echoed in the vacant apartment, almost as though he were playing in a large but totally emptied basilica. Why hadn't I known that he'd actually be tempted by this relic of a piano, or that he'd play a piece I hadn't heard in many years.

It went on for a few minutes and all I wanted was to come behind him and hold his head and kiss him on his exposed nape and ask him to please, please, play it again.

No one seemed to know the piece, and after Paul finished a respectful silence fell over the room. His boyfriend eventually broke through the crowd and placed a very gentle hand on his shoulder, probably to ask him to stop playing, except that Paul suddenly broke out into a Schnittke piece that made everyone laugh. No one knew this piece either, but they all laughed when he right away started playing a madman's rendition of "Bohemian Rhapsody."

Midway through his playing, I had decided to sit on the metal casing covering one of the radiators below a windowsill and Erica came to sit next to me, quietly, like a cat looking to snuggle into a tight spot on a mantelpiece without disturbing or displacing the china. All she did was turn around looking for her husband, and as she did so, let her right elbow lean on my shoulder. He was standing at the other end of the room holding a wine glass in both hands, looking uneasy. She smiled at him. He nodded back. I wondered about them. But after turning to face the piano player she did not remove her elbow from my shoulder. She knew what she was doing. Bold but undecided. But I could focus on nothing else. I admired the carefree ease with one's body that comes from a confident disposition that is used to finding good fellowship everywhere. It reminded me of my younger days when I too assumed that others not only wouldn't mind but actually hoped I'd reach out to touch them. My gratitude for such carefree trust made me reach for the hand closest to my shoulder; I gave it a light, momentary squeeze to thank her for her friendship, knowing that my reaching her hand would displace the elbow. She didn't seem to mind at all, but soon her elbow withdrew. Micol, who'd been in the kitchen, had come to stand next to the radiator and placed her hand on my other shoulder. How different from Erica's elbow.

Paul's boyfriend told him it was time to stop playing as they had to leave soon. "Once he starts playing, there's no stopping, and then I have to be the bully who breaks up the party." At that point, I stood and came up to Paul who was still at the piano, put my arm around him, and said that I had recognized the Arioso by Bach and that I had no idea he was going to play it.

"I didn't know it either," he said, his own sense of surprise at once so disarmingly candid and confiding. He was pleased that I recognized Bach's Capriccio. "It's a piece Bach wrote, 'On the Departure of His Beloved Brother.' You're leaving, so it's not without meaning. If you want I can play it again for you."

What a sweet man, I thought.

"It's because you're leaving," he repeated, and everyone heard, and the sheer humanity in the tone of his voice tore something out of me that I couldn't show or express among so many guests.

So, once again, he played the Arioso. And he was playing it for me, and everyone could see he was playing it for me, and what broke my heart was that I knew, as he must have known, that what is so dreadful about farewells and departures is the near certainty that we'll never see each other again. What he didn't know, and couldn't have known, was that this same Arioso was what I'd heard played for me some twenty years before when, then too, I was the one departing.

Are you listening to his playing? I asked the

one person who was absent, but never absent for me.

I'm listening.

And you know, you do know I've been floundering all these years.

I know. But so have I.

What lovely music you used to play for me.

I wanted to.

So you haven't forgotten.

Of course I haven't.

And while Paul played and I stared at his face and couldn't let go of his eyes that were staring back at me with such unguarded grace and tenderness that I felt it in my gut, I knew that some arcane and beguiling wording was being spoken about what my life had been, and might still be, or might never be, and that the choice rested on the keyboard itself and me.

Paul had just finished playing Bach's Arioso when he immediately explained that he had decided to play a choral prelude as transcribed by Samuil Feinberg. "Less than five minutes, I promise," he said, turning to his partner. "But this tiny choral prelude," he said, interrupting his playing before picking it up again, "can change your life. I think it changes mine each time I play it."

Was he speaking to me?

How could he possibly have known about my life?

But then, he must have known — and I wanted him to know. How music could change my life meant something irreducibly clear the moment he had spoken these words to me, and yet I already sensed that the words themselves would elude me in a matter of seconds, as though their meaning were permanently bound to music, to an evening on the Upper West Side when a young man introduced me to a piece of music that I had never heard before and now wished I'd never stop hearing. Or was it the autumnal night made brighter with the Bach, or was it the loss of this hollowed-out apartment filled with people I'd grown to like and liked even more now because of the consolations of music? Or was music just a premonition of this thing called life, life made more palpable, life made more real — or less real — because there was music and incantation trapped in its folds? Or was it his face, just his face when he had looked up at me from his chair and had said, *If you want I can play it again for you?*

Or perhaps what he might have meant was this: If the music doesn't change you, dear friend, it should at least remind you of something profoundly yours that you've probably lost track of but that actually never went away and still answers when beckoned by the right notes, like a spirit gently roused from a prolonged slumber with the right touch of a finger and the right silence between the notes. *I can play it again for you.* Someone had spoken similar words two decades before: *This is the Bach as transcribed by me.*

As I looked at Erica sitting next to me on the radiator casing and at Paul at the piano I also wanted their lives to be changed because of tonight, because of the music, because of me. Or perhaps all I wanted was for them to bring back something from my past, because it was the past, or something like the past, like memory, or maybe not just memory, but tiers and layers deeper, like life's invisible watermark that I still wasn't seeing.

Then once again his voice. *It's me, isn't it, it's me you're looking for, me the music summons up tonight.*

I looked at the two and could tell they hadn't a clue. I myself didn't have a clue. I could already see how the bridge between the three of us was destined to remain fragile and would so easily be dismantled and drift downstream after tonight, and all the amity and cheer fostered by prosecco, music, and Dr. Chaudhuri's finger food would dissipate. Things might even regress to what they'd been before we discussed toothpastes or laughed at the mean yoga instructor, whose breath, incidentally, was positively foul, wasn't it, she'd said once, as soon as we'd had a moment together after class.

Now, while Paul played, I thought of our home in New Hampshire and how distant and sad everything there seemed as I looked out and faced the nightscape on the Hudson and thought of the furniture that we'd need to uncover once we were home, and the dusting and airing of the house, and all those hasty weekday dinners sitting face-to-face alone now that the boys were away in school. We were close, yet distant too, the reckless fire, the zest, the mad laughter, the dash to Arrigo's Night Bar to order fries and two martinis, how quickly they'd vanished over the years. I had thought marriage would bring us together and that I'd turn over a new leaf. I'd thought that living without children in New York would bring us together again. But I was closer to the music, to the Hudson, to the two of them, about whom I knew not a single thing, and couldn't care a whit about their lives, their Clives, their partners or husbands. Instead, as the choral prelude filled the room and grew a touch louder, my mind drifted elsewhere, as it always does when I've had a bit to drink and hear a piano cutting through an ocean and seas and years away to an old Steinway played by someone who, like a spirit beckoned by Bach tonight, hovered in this barren living room to remind me: *We're still the same, we haven't drifted.* This was how he always spoke to me in such moments, *We're still the same, we haven't drifted* — with a jeering languor inflecting each of his features. He had almost said it five years ago, when he'd come to see me in New Hampshire.

I try to remind him each time that he has no reason to forgive me.

But he utters an impish laugh, shoos away my protestations and, never angry, smiles, takes off his shirt, sits on my lap in his shorts, his thighs straddling mine and his arms tight around my waist while I'm trying to focus on the music and the woman next to me, and raising his face to mine as though about to kiss my lips, whispers, *You fool, it takes two of them to make one of me. I can be man and woman, or both, because you've been both to me. Find me, Oliver. Find me.*

He's visited me many times before but not

like this, not like tonight.

Say something, please tell me something more, I want to say. I could, if I let myself, warm up to him with guarded words and reach out with diffident steps. I've drunk enough tonight to believe he'd love nothing more than to hear from me. The thought thrills me, and the music thrills me, and the young man at the piano thrills me. I want to break our silence.

You've always spoken first. Say something to me. It's almost three a.m. where you are. What are you doing? Are you alone?

Two words from you and everyone's reduced to a stand-in, including me, my life, my work, my home, my friends, my wife, my boys, Greek fire and Greek triremes, and this little romance with Mr. Paul and Ms. Erica, everything becomes a screen, until life itself turns into a diversion.

And all there is, is you.

All I think of is you.

Are you thinking of me tonight? Did I wake you?

He doesn't answer.

"I think you should talk to my friend Karen," said Micol. I crack a joke at Karen's expense. "I also think you've had enough to drink," she snaps.

"And I think I'll have some more," I said, turning to speak with the married specialists on Jewish expatriates from the Third Reich and, without knowing how it happened, began to laugh. What on earth were these two doing in my soon to be ex-home?

Holding another glass of prosecco, I did walk up to and speak with Micol's friend. But then seeing the scholars on Jewish expatriates from the Third Reich I found myself laughing again.

Obviously I'd had too much to drink.

I was thinking of my wife again and of my boys away in school. At home, every day, she'll sit finishing her book. Then she'll let me read it, she says, when we're back in our small college town wearing snow boots all through the school year, teaching in snow boots, going to the movies in snow boots, to dinners, to faculty meetings, to the bathroom, to our bed in snow boots, and all of this tonight will be a thing from another era. Erica a thing of the past, and Paul locked in the past as well, and I'll be no more than a shadow clutching to this very wall that won't see me tomorrow, still not letting go, like a fly struggling against the draft that must whoosh it away. Would they remember?

Paul asked why I was laughing.

"I must be happy," I said. "Or it's too much prosecco."

"Me too."

It made the three of us laugh.

I remembered that after the Arioso and the choral prelude, after the endless toasts and all the prosecco, there had been a moment of awkwardness when I helped Erica find her cardigan in the guest room. Two of the guests had already left, the others had congregated in the hallway, waiting. We were alone in the room, and, as I told her how happy I was that she had come, I could have let the silence between us last a little longer. I sensed her unease but knew she wouldn't have minded a few more seconds of this. But I decided not to push things any further and instead found myself kissing her goodbye on her exposed neck instead of her cheek. She smiled, as I smiled. My smile was apology, hers forbearance.

When it came time to bid him goodbye, I made a gesture to shake his hand, but he embraced me even before my hand touched his. I liked his shoulder blades when we hugged. Then he kissed me on both cheeks. His boyfriend kissed me the same way as well.

I was pleased, thrilled, and crushed. I

stood at the door and watched all four of them walk down the corridor. I'd never see them again.

What had I wanted from them? For them to like each other so I could sit, sip more prosecco, and then decide whether or not to join their party? Or had I liked them both and couldn't decide which of the two I wanted more? Or did I want neither but needed to think I did because otherwise I'd have to look into my life and find huge, bleak craters everywhere going back to that scuttled, damaged love I'd told them about earlier that evening.

Micol and her friend Karen were cleaning up in the kitchen. I'd told them to leave the dishes alone. Karen reminded me point-blank that she'd like to speak to me again. "Maybe soon?" she said. "As soon as I'm back in the city," I said. I lied.

Micol walked her to the elevator then came back, meaning to help tidy up a bit before turning in. I told her not to bother.

"Nice party," she said.

"Very nice."

"So, who were those two?"

"Kids."

She gave me a knowing smile. "I'm going to bed, are you coming?"

I had cleaning up to do, I said, but I'd

join her soon enough.

I took my time putting some of the plastic dishes into two contractor bags left over from our packing and, as I was about to turn off the lights in the living room, I found a pack of cigarettes on the side table near the only ashtray in the apartment, probably Karen's. I took one out of the pack, lit it, turned off all the lights, put the ashtray next to me on the old sofa that was no longer ours, put my feet up on one of the four chairs that would stay behind with their new masters, and began thinking of the Arioso as I remembered hearing it so long ago. Then in the semi-darkened living room I looked out and caught the full moon. My God, how beautiful it was. And the more I stared at it, the more I longed to speak to it.

Didn't change your life, did I? says good old Johann Sebastian.

Afraid not.

And why not?

Music doesn't give answers to questions I don't know how to ask. It doesn't tell me what I want. It reminds me that I may still be in love, though I'm no longer sure I know what that means, being in love. I think about people all the time, yet I've hurt many more than I've cared for. I can't even tell what I feel, though feel something I still do, even if it's more like a sense of absence and loss, maybe even failure, numbness, or total unknowing. I was sure of myself once, I thought I knew things, knew myself, and people loved that I reached out to touch them when I blustered into their lives and didn't even ask or doubt that I mightn't be welcome. Music reminds me of what my life should have been. But it doesn't change me.

Perhaps, says the genius, music doesn't change us that much, nor does great art change us. Instead, it reminds us of who, despite all our claims or denials, we've always known we were and are destined to remain. It reminds us of the mileposts we've buried and hidden and then lost, of the people and things that mattered despite our lies, despite the years. Music is no more than the sound of our regrets put to a cadence that stirs the illusion of pleasure and hope. It's the surest reminder that we're here for a very short while and that we've neglected or cheated or, worse yet, failed to live our lives. Music is the unlived life. You've lived the wrong life, my friend, and almost defaced the one you were given to live.

What do I want? Do you know the answer, Herr Bach? Is there such a thing as a right or wrong life?

I'm an artist, my friend, I don't do answers.

Artists know questions only. And besides, you already know the answer.

In a better world, she'd be sitting next to me on the sofa to my left, and he'd be at my right, an inch away from the ashtray. She kicks off her shoes and puts her feet up next to mine, on the coffee table. *My feet,* she finally says, sensing we're all staring at them. *Ugly feet, aren't they?* she says. *Not ugly at all,* I say. I'm holding their hands. I free one hand, but only to let it linger on his forehead. While she leans into my shoulder, he turns around, faces me, then kisses me on the mouth. It's a long, deep kiss. Neither of us minds that she's watching. I want her to watch. The kid kisses well. She says nothing at first, then, *I want him to kiss me too.* He smiles at her, and almost climbing over me kisses her on the mouth. Afterward she says she likes the way he kisses. *Agreed,* I say. *But he smells of cigarettes. My fault,* I say. *You didn't like the smell?* he asks. *I liked it fine,* she replies. I kiss her. She doesn't complain that I smell of tobacco. I'm thinking, *Fennel.* I want her to taste of his fennel, from his mouth to her mouth to my mouth, and back to his.

Later that night, I went to sleep thinking of the three of us naked in bed. We are hugging, but in the end the two are curled up against me, each with a thigh on one of mine. How easily it might have happened, and so naturally, as though both had come to dinner with little else in mind. Why so many schemes, and so much planning, and such anxieties when, hours earlier, I was standing the bottles in buckets of ice. I loved the thought of his sweat and hers mingled with mine. Yet all I ended up focusing on was their Achilles tendons. Hers, when she'd removed her shoes and put both feet on the coffee table, his when he walked in at the very start of the evening and I spotted him wearing boat shoes without socks. I had no idea how slim and smooth and delicate his feet were. Later, he too had taken off his shoes before placing both feet on the coffee table, one slim, tanned ankle over the other. *Look at mine,* he'd said, twitching the toes of one foot. We laughed. *Boys' feet,* she said. *I know,* he replied. Once again he moved closer, placed a knee on my thigh, and kissed me.

I don't recall what I dreamed that night, but I know that, all through the night and through countless flushed and fitful reawakenings, I had loved the two of them, together or separately I couldn't tell, because there was something so thoroughly real in their unhindered presence in my arms that when

I woke in the middle of the night clutching my wife, I felt, as I'd already imagined earlier that evening, that it wouldn't be far-fetched to start preparing breakfast for the four of us in a kitchen that reminded me of a house in Italy.

I thought of Micol. She had no place in this. Italy was a chapter we never discussed. But she knew. She knew that one day — she just knew, and probably better than I did. I had once wanted to tell her about my old friends, and their house by the sea, and of my room there, and about the lady of the house, who years ago was like a mother to me but who now had dementia and hardly remembered her own name, and about her husband who, before dying, lived in the same house with another woman, who still lives there with a seven-year-old son I'm dying to meet.

I need to go back, Micol.

Why?

Because my life stopped there. Because I never really left. Because the rest of me here has been like the severed tail of a lizard that flays and lashes about, while the body's stayed behind all the way across the Atlantic in that wonderful house by the sea. I've been away for far too long.

Are you leaving me?

318

I think so.
And the children too?
I'll always be their father.
And when is this happening?
I don't know. Soon.
I can't say I'm surprised.
I know.

That same night, after the guests had left and Micol had gone to bed, I turned off the light in the entrance and was about to shut the French windows to the balcony when I remembered to blow out the candles. I stepped outside again, stood facing the river, placed both hands on the banister where I'd stood with Erica and Paul earlier in the evening, and stared out across the water. I liked the lights across the Hudson, I liked the fresh breeze, I liked Manhattan this time of year, I liked the sight of the George Washington Bridge, which I knew I'd miss once I was back in New Hampshire but that right now, on this night, still reminded me of Monte Carlo when its sparkling lights reach into Italy at night. Soon, it would be cold on the Upper West Side and there would be days of rain, but the weather always cleared eventually here and people still milled about the streets late at night when it was cold in this city that never sleeps.

I slid the deck chairs back into their place, picked up a half-empty wine glass from the floor, and spotted another, which had been used as an ashtray and was brimming with butts. How many had been smoking outside? The yoga teacher, Karen, Micol herself, the married couple I'd met at the conference on Jewish expatriates from the Third Reich, the vegans, who else?

Now, as I admired the view and kept watching two tugboats gliding quietly upstream, I thought that one day fifty years from now someone else would surely step outside on this very balcony and stand here admiring this same view, nursing similar thoughts, but it wouldn't be me. Would he be in his teens or his eighties, or would he be my own age now, and would he, like me, still long for an old and only love, trying not to think of some unknown soul who, just like me tonight some fifty years before, had longed for a beloved and tried, as I caught myself trying and failing after all these years, not to give it a thought.

The past, the future, what masks they are.

And what screens those two were, Erica and Paul.

Everything was a screen, and life itself was a diversion.

What mattered now was unlived.

I looked up at the moon and meant to ask about my life. But her answer came far sooner than I was able to formulate the question. *For twenty years you've lived a dead man's life. Everyone knows. Even your wife and your children and your wife's friend, and the couple you met at a conference on the Jewish expatriates from the Third Reich can read it on your face. Erica and Paul know it, and those scholars who study Greek fire and Greek triremes, even the Pre-Socratics themselves, dead two thousand years ago, can tell. The only one who doesn't know is you. But now even you know.*

You've been disloyal.

To what, to whom? To yourself.

I remembered that a few days earlier, while shopping for boxes and tape, I'd spotted someone I knew across the street. I waved at him but he didn't wave back and kept walking, though I knew he'd seen me. Maybe he was upset with me. But upset about what? Moments later I saw someone from my department headed to a bookstore. We crossed paths by one of the fruit vendors on the sidewalk and, though he too looked in my direction, he failed to return my smile. A while later I saw a neighbor from my building on the sidewalk; we normally exchange pleasantries in the elevator, but she didn't say anything or nod back when I acknowledged her. It suddenly occurred to me that the only explanation was that I had died and that this was what death was like: you see people but they don't see you, and worse yet, you're trapped being who you were in the moment you died — buying corrugated boxes — and you never changed into the one person you could have been and knew you really were, and you never redressed the one mistake that threw your life off course and now you were forever trapped doing the very last stupid thing you were doing, buying corrugated boxes and tape. I was forty-four years old. I was already dead — and yet too young, too young to die.

After shutting the windows, I thought of Bach's Arioso again and began to hum it in my head. In moments such as these, when we are all alone and our mind is altogether elsewhere, facing eternity and ready to take stock of this thing called our life and of all we've done or half done or left undone, what would my answer be to the questions good old Bach said I already knew the answer to?

One person, one name — he knows, I

thought. Right now, he knows, he still knows.

Find me, he says.

I will, Oliver, I will, I say. Or has he forgotten?

But he remembers what I've just done. He looks at me, says nothing, I can tell he's moved.

And suddenly, with the Arioso still in my mind and yet another glass and another of Karen's cigarettes, I wanted him to play this Arioso for me, followed by the choral prelude, which he'd never played before, and to play it for me, just for me. And the more I thought of his playing, the more the tears began to well in my eyes, and it didn't matter if it was the alcohol still speaking or my heart, for all I wanted was to hear him now, playing this Arioso on his parents' Steinway on a rainy summer's night in their house by the sea, and I would sit close to the piano with a glass of something and I'd be with him and no longer be so thoroughly alone as I've been for so many, many years, alone among strangers who did not know a thing about me or about him. I would ask him to play the Arioso and by playing it to remind me of this very night when I snuffed out the candles on the balcony, turned off the lights in the living room, lit a cigarette, and for once in my life knew where I wanted to be and what I had to do.

It would happen as it did the first time or the second or third. Make up a reason that's believable enough to others and to myself, take a plane, rent a car, or hire someone to take me there, drive up the old familiar roads, which have probably changed over the years or maybe not so much, and that still remember me as I remember them, and before I know it, there it is: the old pine alley, the familiar sound of pebbles crunching under the tires as the car slows to a halt, and then the house. I look up, I think there's no one, they don't know I'm coming, although I've written that I am, but sure enough, there he is, waiting. I've told him not to wait up. *Of course I'll wait up,* he replies, and in that *Of course,* all our years rush back, because there's a trace of muted irony, which was how he spoke his heart when we were together, meaning *You know I'll always wait up, even if you get here at four a.m. All these years, I've waited up, do you think I won't wait up a few more hours now?*

Waiting up is what we've done all our lives, waiting up allows me to stand here remembering Bach's music playing at my end of our planet and letting my thoughts go out to you, for all I want is to think of you, and sometimes

I don't know who's the one thinking, you or I.

I'm here, he says.

Did I wake you?

Yes.

Do you mind?

No.

Are you alone?

Does it matter? But yes.

He says he's changed. He hasn't.

I still run.

Me too.

And I drink a bit more.

Ditto.

But sleep poorly.

Ditto.

Anxiety, a touch of depression.

Ditto, ditto.

You're coming back, aren't you?

How did you know?

I know, Elio.

When? Elio asks.

In a couple of weeks.

I want you to.

You think?

I know.

I won't come up the tree-lined alley as I'd planned. Instead, the plane will land in Nice.

I'll pick you up by car, then. It will be late morning. Same as the first time.

You remember.

I remember.

And I want to see the boy.

Did I ever tell you his name? My father named him after you. Oliver. He never forgot you.

It will be hot and there'll be no shade. But the scent of rosemary will be everywhere, and I'll recognize the cooing of turtledoves and behind the house there'll be a field of wild lavender and sunflowers raising their befuddled big heads at the sun. The swimming pool, the belfry nicknamed To-Die-For, the monument to the dead soldiers of the Piave, the tennis court, the rickety gate that leads down to the rocky beach, the whetting stone in the afternoon, the unending rattle of cicadas, me and you, your body and mine.

If he asks how long I'm staying, I'll tell him the truth.

If he asks where I plan to sleep, I'll tell him the truth.

If he asks.

But he won't ask. He won't have to. He knows.

DA CAPO

"Why Alexandria?" Oliver asked as we stopped along the esplanade, watching the sun set beyond the breakwater on our first evening there. The smell of fish, salt, and bracken-still water along the shoreline was overpowering, yet we continued to stand on that stretch of the walkway across from the home of our Alexandrian Greek hosts, staring at the spot where everyone said the old lighthouse once stood. Our hosts' family had lived here for eight generations — the lighthouse, they insisted, couldn't have been located anywhere else but on the spot where the fortress of Qaitbey stands. But no one knew for sure. Meanwhile, the fading sun was in our eyes, and its color stained the distance with large brushstrokes that were not pink or subdued orange but bright, loud tangerine. Neither of us had seen that color in the sky before.

Why Alexandria? could have meant so

many things: from *Why is this place as it stands now so central to the history of the West?* down to something as whimsical as *Why did we choose to come here?* I'd wanted to reply, *Because everything that's meant anything to either of us — Ephesus, Athens, Syracuse — probably ended here.* I was thinking of the Greeks, of Alexander and his lover Hephaestion, of the Library, and Hypatia, and ultimately of the modern Greek poet Cavafy. But I also knew why he was asking.

We'd left the house in Italy for a three-week tour of the Mediterranean. Our ship stopped in Alexandria for two nights and we were enjoying our last few days before sailing back home. We had wanted to be alone together. Too many people in the house. My mother, who had come to live with us and couldn't use the stairs any longer, now lived in a room on the ground floor not far enough from ours. Then there was her caregiver. Then Miranda, who stayed in my old bedroom when she wasn't traveling. And finally Little Ollie, whose room, next to hers, had once belonged to my grandfather. We shared my parents' old bedroom. I'm sure everyone could hear if you so much as coughed at night.

Nor had it been as easy in Italy as we'd

expected at first. We knew things were going to be different but we couldn't quite grasp how the wish to rush headlong into what we'd once had years before could stir our reluctance to be in bed together. We were in the same house where it had all started — but were we the same? He tried blaming jet lag, and I let him, while he turned his back as I turned off the light before removing my clothes. I mistook the fear of being disappointed for the far more troubling fear of disappointing him. I knew he was thinking along the same lines when he finally turned around and said, "Elio, I haven't made love to a man in so many years," adding, as he laughed, "I may have forgotten how." We'd hoped desire might foil our diffidence, but the sense of awkwardness wasn't going away. At some point in the dark, feeling the strain between us, I even suggested that perhaps talking might dispel what was holding us back. Was I being unwittingly distant, I asked. No, not distant at all. Was I being difficult? Difficult? No. Then what was it?

"Time," he replied. As always, this was all he said. Did he need time, I asked, almost ready to move far away from him on our bed. No, he replied.

It took me a while to understand that what he'd meant was that too much time had gone by.

"Just hug me," I finally said.

"And see where that goes?" he immediately quipped, inflecting each word with irony. I could tell he was nervous.

"Yes, and see where that goes," I echoed. I remembered the afternoon when I'd visited him in his class five years earlier and he'd touched my cheek with his palm. I would have slept with him in no time if he'd asked. So why hadn't he? "Because you would have laughed at me. Because you might have said no. Because I wasn't sure you'd forgiven me."

We didn't make love that night, but falling asleep in his arms and hearing him breathe, and recognizing the scent of his breath after so many years and knowing that I was finally in bed with my Oliver without either of us moving away as we released our hold, was exactly what made me realize that despite two decades we were not a day older than the two young men we'd been so long ago under this same roof. In the morning he gave me a look. I didn't want silence to bridge the gap. I wanted him to speak. But he wasn't going to speak.

"Is this morning . . . or is this for me?" I finally asked. "Because right now mine's real."

"Same here," he said.

And it was I, not he, who remembered how he liked it started. "I've only done this with you," he said, confirming what we both knew was happening between us. "But I'm still nervous," he added.

"I've never known you to be."

"I know."

"I must tell you something too —" I started because I wanted him to know.

"What?"

"I've saved all this for you."

"What if we were never to be together again?"

"That was never going to happen." Then I couldn't help myself: "You know what I like."

"I know."

"So you didn't forget."

He smiled. No, he hadn't.

At dawn, after sex, we went swimming as we'd done years earlier.

When we returned the house was still sleeping.

"I'll make coffee."

"I would love coffee," he said.

"Miranda likes it Neapolitan style. We've been brewing coffee that way for ages now."

"Fine" was his send-off as he headed to the shower. After filling the coffeepot I started boiling water for the eggs. I put down two place mats, one on the long side of the kitchen table, the other at the head. Then I put four slices of bread in the toaster but didn't start it. By the time he was back, I told him to watch for the coffee but not to turn over the pot once the coffee was ready. I loved his hair when it was combed but still wet. I'd forgotten that look in the morning. Not two hours earlier we weren't quite sure we'd ever make love again. I stopped fiddling with breakfast and looked at him. He knew what I was thinking and smiled. Yes, the unease that had scared us was behind us now, and as though to confirm this, before leaving the kitchen to take a shower, I placed a lingering kiss on his neck. "I haven't been kissed like that in so long," he said. "Time," I said, using his word to rib him.

After I'd showered and was back in the kitchen, to my surprise I found Oliver and Oliver seated next to each other on the long side of the table. I dropped six eggs in the boiling water for the three of us. As they discussed a film we'd seen the night before on television, it was clear that Little Ollie had taken an instant liking to Oliver.

I buttered the warm toast for everyone and watched Oliver cut off the top of the eggshell for Little Ollie and then his as well. "You know who taught me how to do this?" he asked.

"Who?" asked the boy.

"Your brother. Every morning he used to cut the egg for me. Because I didn't know how it was done. They don't teach you this in America. I've been cutting the eggs for my two sons as well."

"You have sons?"

"Yes, I do."

"What are their names?"

He told him.

"And do you know whom you're named after?" Oliver finally asked.

"Yes."

"Who?"

"You."

As soon as I heard these last few words, something tightened in my throat. This underscored so many things we hadn't said, or hadn't had time to say, or couldn't find the words to say, yet here it was, like a final chord resolving an unfinished melodic air. So much time had passed, so many years, and who knew how many of them might turn out to have been the wasted years that, unbeknownst to us, end up making us better people. No wonder I was moved. The child was like our child, and seemed so

335

emphatically prophesied that everything suddenly became clear to me — because there was a reason for the boy's name, because Oliver had always been of my blood and had always lived in this house, been of this house and of our lives. He was already here before coming to us, before my birth, before they set down the first stone generations ago, and our years in between then and now were but a hiccup in that long itinerary called time. So much time, so many years, and all the lives we'd touched and left behind, as though they could just as easily have never happened, though happen they did — time, as he'd said before we hugged and went to sleep so late that night, time is always the price we pay for the unlived life.

And as I was pouring his coffee and hovering behind him it crossed my mind that I shouldn't have showered after this morning's lovemaking, that I wanted every trace of him still on me, because we hadn't even spoken about what we'd done at dawn yet and I wanted to hear him repeat what he'd said to me while we were making love. I wanted to tell him about our night, and how I was sure neither of us had slept as soundly as we'd claimed. Without speech, our night could so easily disappear, as he himself could just as easily disappear. I don't know what seized me, but after I poured his coffee, I lowered my voice and almost kissed his earlobe. "You're never going back," I whispered. "Tell me you're not leaving."

Quietly, he grabbed my arm and pulled me down to my seat at the head of the table. "I'm not leaving. Stop thinking like that."

I wanted to tell him about what had happened twenty years before, the good, the bad, the very good, and the terrible. There'd be time to say these things. I wanted to bring him up-to-date, to let him know everything, as I wanted to know everything about him. I wanted to tell him how on seeing the white of his arms on his very first day among us, all I'd wanted was to be held by them and to feel them on my bare waist. I'd told him some of this while we lay in bed hours earlier. "You'd been on an archaeological dig in Sicily, and your arms were so tanned, I noticed them for the first time in our dining room — but the undersides of your arms were so white, and streaked with veins, like marble, and they seemed so delicate. I wanted to kiss each arm, and lick each arm." "Even then?" "Even then. Will you just hug me now?" "And see where that goes?" he'd asked, and it was good we'd held each other and hadn't done anything more that night. He must have read my thoughts, because this was when he put an arm over my shoulder, brought me close to him, and, turning to the boy, said: "Your brother is such a wonderful person."

The boy looked at us. "You think?"

"Don't you think so?"

"Yes, I do." The boy smiled. He knew, as I knew and Oliver knew, that irony was the language of the house.

And then without warning, the boy asked: "Are you a good person too?"

Even Oliver was moved and had to catch his breath. The child was our child. The two of us knew it. And my father, who no longer was alive, knew it just as well, had known all along.

"Can you believe that the old lighthouse stood here, that we are standing hardly a ten-minute walk away from it?"

We were in Alexandria for another night, then headed for Naples — our gift to ourselves, or as Miranda called it, our honeymoon, before Oliver was to start teaching at the Sapienza, in Rome. But as we stood staring at the sun and watching families, friends, and people stroll along the esplanade, I wanted to ask if he remembered the moment when we'd sat on a rock one evening and looked out to the sea days before he was to return to New York. Yes, he remembered, he said, of course he remembered. I asked if he recalled the nights we'd spent in Rome exploring the city into the wee hours. Yes, he remembered that too. I was going to say that that trip had changed my life, not only because we had spent our time in total freedom together, but because Rome had allowed me to taste the life of an artist, which I craved but didn't know I was meant to live. We got so drunk yet hardly slept that first night in Rome. And we met so many poets, artists, editors, actors. But then he stopped me. "We're not going to feed off the past, are we?" he asked in his usual laconic manner that told me I had strayed into territory that held no promise for the future. He couldn't have been more right. "I've had to sever many ties and burn bridges I know I'll pay dearly for, but I don't want to look back. I've had Micol, you've had Michel, just as I've loved a young Elio and you a younger me. They've made us who we are. Let's not pretend they never existed, but I don't want to look back."

Earlier that day we had been to Cavafy's home on what was once rue Lepsius, later renamed rue Sharm el Sheikh, and now known as rue C. P. Cavafy. We laughed at the change of street names, at how the city, so inexorably ambivalent since the dawn of its founding three hundred and some years before Christ, couldn't even make up its mind what to call its own streets. "Everything comes in layers here," I said. He didn't respond.

What surprised me as soon as we walked into the sultry apartment that had once been the great poet's home was hearing Oliver rattle off his greeting to the attendant in perfect Greek. How and when had he learned modern Greek? And how many more things didn't I know about his life, and how many didn't he know about mine? He'd taken a crash course, he said, but what truly helped was the sabbatical he'd spent in Greece with his wife and sons. The boys acquired the language in no time, while his wife had stayed home a lot, reading the Durrell brothers on a sunlit deck and picking up snippets of Greek from their cleaning lady, who spoke no English.

Cavafy's apartment, which was now a makeshift museum, felt drab and desultory despite the open windows. The neighborhood itself was drab. There was scant light as we entered and, with the exception of scattered sounds rising from the street, the dead silence in the home sat heavily on the spare, old furniture that had most likely been picked up from some abandoned storage house. Yet the apartment reminded me of one of my favorite poems by the poet, about a band of afternoon sunlight falling across a bed in which the poet, in his younger days, used to sleep with his lover. Now, as the poet revisits the premises years later, all the furniture is gone, the bed is gone, and the apartment has been turned into a business office. But that ray of sunlight that was once spread over the bed has not left him and stays forever in his memory. His lover had said he'd be back within a week; but he never returned. I felt the poet's sorrow. One seldom recovers.

We were both disappointed by the assortment of cheaply made photo-portraits of a grim-looking Cavafy that lined the walls. To commemorate the visit, we bought a volume of poems in Greek. When we sat next to each other in an old Greek pastry shop overlooking the bay, Oliver began reading aloud one of the poems to me, first in Greek and then in his own hasty translation. I couldn't remember reading that poem before. It was about a Greek colony in Italy that the Greeks called Poseidonia and that was later renamed Paistos by the Lucanians and still later Paestum by the Romans. Over the centuries and so many generations after they'd settled, these Greeks eventually lost the memory of their Greek heritage and of the Greek language, and acquired Italianate customs instead — except for one day each year when, on that ritual anniversary, the Poseidonians would celebrate a Greek festival with Greek music and Greek rites to recall, as best each could, the forgotten customs and language of their forebears, realizing to their profound sorrow that they'd lost their magnificent Greek heritage and were no better than the Barbarians the Greeks were wont to scorn. By sundown that day they'd be cradling the very scraps of their residual Greek identity only to watch it vanish by sunup the next day.

It was then, as we ate the sweet pastries, that it occurred to Oliver that just like the Poseidonians, the few remaining Alexandrian Greeks today — our hosts, the attendant in the museum, the very old waiter in our pastry shop, the man who had sold us an English-language newspaper this morning — all had acquired new customs, new habits, and spoke a language that smacked of obsolescence compared to the Greek spoken nowadays on the mainland.

But Oliver told me something I will never forget: that on the sixteenth of November each year — my birthday — though married and the father of two sons, he would take time out to remember the Poseidonian in himself and to consider what life would have been had we stayed together. "I feared I was starting to forget your face, your voice, your smell, even," he said. Over the years he had found his own ritual spot not far from his office, overlooking a lake where he would take a few moments on that day to think of our unlived life, his with mine. The vigil, as my father would have called it, never lasted long enough and it disrupted nothing. But recently, he went on, and perhaps because he was elsewhere that year, it came to him that the situation was entirely reversed, that he was a Poseidonian on all but one day a year and that the lure of bygone days had never left him, that he had forgotten nothing and didn't want to forget, and that even if he couldn't write or call to see whether I too had forgotten nothing, still, he knew that though neither of us sought out the other it was only because we had never really parted and that, regardless of where we were, who we were with, and whatever stood in our way, all he needed when the time was right was simply to come and find me.

"And you did."

"And I did," he said.

"I wish my father were alive today."

Oliver looked at me, was silent a while, then said: "So do I, so do I."

ABOUT THE AUTHOR

André Aciman is the author of *Eight White Nights, Call Me by Your Name, Out of Egypt, False Papers, Alibis, Harvard Square,* and *Enigma Variations,* and is the editor of *The Proust Project.* He teaches comparative literature at the Graduate Center of the City University of New York. He lives with his wife in Manhattan.